CW00736188
POST CARD
NATIONAL
War Bonds are Victory Bonds
SAVINGS
A full list of subscriptions to
will be kept at
Street, London, E.C.
tion during business hours.
Y.M.C.A.
CARTE POSTALE
Correspondance
April 18/15
Dear Tom
To the Secretary
ANTI-GERMAN LEAGUE,
25, Victoria Street,
Westminster
S.W.
RETURN TO
STALE
ADRESSE
PASSED
Imp. G. Savigny, Paris, — P. 6

It'll All Be Over By Christmas

It'll All Be Over By Christmas

THE FIRST WORLD WAR IN POSTCARDS

John Wilton

A donation from the proceeds of the sale of this book will be given by the author to the Gurkha Welfare Trust who support Gurkha veterans, their widows and the wider community across Nepal.

This edition first published in the UK by Uniform
an imprint of Unicorn Publishing Group, 2022
Charleston Studio
Meadow Business Centre
Lewes BN8 5RW

www.unicornpublishing.org

10 9 8 7 6 5 4 3 2 1

ISBN 978-1-914414-98-5

Cover design by Unicorn Publishing Group
Typeset by Vivian Head

Printed by Gutenberg Press, Malta

Contents

Introduction

POSTCARDS USED BETWEEN August 1914 and the end of 1919 can be roughly divided into two categories: those sent from a postal address in Great Britain to another address in Great Britain, and those sent from the Western Front, the Middle East or Italy to Great Britain. A few cards do not fit into the above categories and include those sent to or from Canada, Africa or the USA.

During the war years, many cards were used that did not feature the war, but rather town and village scenes and days by the seaside. Others, however, were part of a massive propaganda campaign. The British government's task was first to persuade the population that the war was just – neutral Belgium had been invaded by Germany, and Great Britain had signed a treaty to guarantee Belgium's neutrality. They then had to persuade the population that they should fight or support the war effort in other ways.

There was also a plan to portray the 'enemy' as both evil and ridiculous. The Kaiser and his son 'Little Willie' were singled out for ridicule. The aim was then to forecast that victory would be achieved because 'our Navy ruled the waves' and our Commonwealth would join the 'mother country' in her hour of need.

Communications between Britain and the war zones were usually by letter. Those between the war zones and home were by letter, postcards enclosed in an envelope, or by postcard. Soldiers writing cards from the front frequently promised to write a letter later when they had more time.

Hear Ye Nations! Why Britain went to War.

Extract from Article 7 of the International Treaty of 1839—renewed in 1870.

"Belgium within the limits specified in Articles I. II. and IV. shall form an independent and perpetually Neutral State."

British Honour *versus* German Dishonour.

"We are fighting to vindicate the principle that small Nationalities are not to be crushed, in defiance of International good faith, by the arbitrary will of a strong and over-mastering Power."

Premier HERBERT H. ASQUITH, in the British House of Commons, August 6th, 1914.

Read this in Contrast :—

"Gentlemen, we are now in a state of necessity, and necessity knows no law! The wrong that we are committing—I speak openly—we will endeavour to make good as soon as **our Military goal has been reached.**"

Chancellor VON BETHMAN-HOLLWEG, in the Reichstag, August 4th, 1914.

Palmerston (Britain)

(Belgium)

(Austria)

(France)

Germany)

(Russia)

PLATE 1 THE NEUTRALITY OF BELGIUM IS NOT RESPECTED

The card depicts German artillery passing through the town of Theux, near Spa, Belgium on 8 August 1914. It was was sent from Aldershot to Miss Lewis, 56 Union Street. Aldershot.

PLATE 2 HEAR YE NATIONS! WHY BRITAIN WENT TO WAR

1 War Declared

The British declaration of war came on 5 August 2014 at 12.15 a.m. when the Foreign Office released the following statement:

> Owing to the summary rejection by the German Government of the request made by His Majesty's Government for assurances that the neutrality of Belgium will be respected, His Majesty's Ambassador at Berlin has received his passports and His Majesty's Government have declared to the German Government that a state of war exists between Great Britain and Germany as from 11pm on August 4th.[1]

PLATE 2

The card in the H.E.R. Rogers Series 31, Great St Helens, London was not postally used but would have been printed at the start of hostilities.

Britain's small, highly trained, regular army was no match in terms of numbers for the huge German force which, within a week of mobilisation, had 3.1 million men under arms. Lord Kitchener foresaw that a new 'citizens' army would be required, made up of volunteers.

The British government had envisaged that, in terms of war, the regular and territorial armies would simply grow organically, taking on recruits and expanding as required. Lord Kitchener, who had little enough faith in the prowess of the new Territorial Force, decided to discard the idea and, as the new Secretary of State for War, create an entirely new army of 100,000 men. However, such was the apparent enthusiasm to fight that three times that number of civilians enlisted in

August before word even got out that this new army was needed. Then, when Kitchener launched his famous appeal, epitomised by the poster 'Your Country Needs You', there came a second, spontaneous response, with hundreds of thousands of men besieging recruiting stations set up right across the country.[2]

PLATE 3 LONDON 1914
The card, not postally used, depicts a scene in London in 1914.

PLATE 4 'DUTY'S CALL WILL ALWAYS FIND ME READY, YE KEN!'

The card was postmarked 2.15 p.m., 4 August 1914 and sent from Dundee, Scotland to Mrs A. Innes in Nairn.

> 'Arrived home all safe last night I don't think I have to go off to Aberdeen I think I will be one the Dunkeld Rd Perth but am waiting word. Will'

It seems 'Will' thought that there could be a recruiting station set up on the Perth to Dunkeld Road, now the A9.

PLATE 5 THE SEA IS ENGLAND'S GLORY

The card was sent from Paisley on 4 September 1914 by Hugh to Miss Jennie Dryburn, Mossbank, Ardbeg, Rothesay (on the Isle of Bute).

> 'Dear Jenny, I have passed the D – and leave on Monday forenoon for Aberdeen, I shall try and take a run over either tomorrow or Sunday Love from Hugh.'

PLATE 6 MOBILISATION OF THE CROYDON TERRITORIALS, AUGUST 1914

PLATE 6

The card was written on 11 August 1914 but not postally used; it may have been sent enclosed in an envelope.

> 'My dear girl,
> I thought you would like to have this card showing some of our Croydon troops off to do their duty for their King & Country there are only a few of them leaving the barracks in Mitcham Rd. Am looking forward to seeing you also Aunt. With much love from us all your loving Mother.'

The Corporal standing on the left of the photograph is one of several soldiers wearing the Overseas Service Commitment badge, worn by all territorial soldiers who volunteered to serve overseas.

PLATE 7 TERRIERS
Territorial forces were known as Terriers. Here, three stand ready to defend their country. The card by Bamforth & Co Ltd. in the War Cartoons series was posted from Wallasey on 24 January 1915.

PLATE 8 ARRIVAL OF THE K.O.R.'S LYDD (KENT), 1914

PLATE 8
The card was not postally used. Boys, including one on a bicycle, accompany the troops as they march along Lydd High Street, probably to a camp located to the south of the village. The wind section of the band is playing and an officer is seen on horseback.

The British Army, backed by Territorial personnel, were dispatched to France without delay. But for the volunteers, a million of whom joined in the first three months after the declaration of war, there was much training to undergo. In many cases, it took a full year for the new civilian soldiers to be fully trained and, although some volunteers left for France in 1915, most Kitchener men would not see action until the following year.

PLATE 9 DON'T WORRY, WE'LL SOON BE BACK

No one wanted to contemplate a war lasting beyond Christmas 1914. Sadly, they were to be disappointed. The card above is not dated or postmarked.

'Dear Mother,
We are now in civilization at Babworth near Retford (Notts.) Only we who are going away have come today. I think the others are coming tomorrow. I think we shall be off sometime this weekend just our luck when we have got to a nice place.
Kind regards Dyson'

Many cards depict sad partings.

PLATE 10 I WONDER IF HE WILL EVER COME BACK

Some cards expressed rather more sombre thoughts. E. Brett writes from Windmill Hill Camp B—— on 29 July 1915 to Private F. Hullat, no. 1 Hut, Cambridge Hospital, Aldershot, Hants.

> 'Dear old Pal just a card hoping you are getting better but you wont be able to come with the boys as we are off to France tomorrow old Pigeon and the rest all wish to be remembered to you with love E. Brett.'

PLATE 11 'KEEP A SMILING FACE'

PLATE 11

'Keep a smiling face
Keep a heart that's true
And in your heart for me a place
When I come back to you!'

This Donald McGill card in the Comique series is not dated or postmarked. Herbert writes:

> 'Memory's that lives is the dear girl I cherish xxxxxx To my Dear Dolly with much love Herbert.'

PLATE 12

This card, neither dated nor postally used, depicts a father saying goodbye to his wife and family. Families whose male parent had gone to war would have been entitled to separation allowances, to offset the loss of income. The rate was 12s. 6d. (62p) per week, with an extra 2s. (10p) for each child. So the family featured above would have received 12s. 6d. (62p) and seven times 2s. (70p), a total of £1 6s. 6d. (£1.32). The amount rarely compensated the family for the financial loss. A private's pay was 7s. (35p) a week, which corresponded to 1s. a day (otherwise known as the 'king's shilling').

PLATE 12 IT TAKES A LONG TIME TO SAY GOODBYE

PLATE 13 'SAY AU REVOIR, BUT NOT GOOD-BYE!'

The card was sent from Redcar on 15 February 1915 to Miss D. Sampson, c/o Mr Cliff, no. 74 Marsh Lane, Leeds. On it, a young cavalry officer, with spurs on his boots, is depicted saying goodbye to his lady.

'Dear Dot,
I arrived here in good time and quick well I know you will excuse card, because I have had to go in the trenches and we are now busy getting ready to move. I am writing letters tomorrow old love, we have not got paid yet they have changed payday to Saturday. So cheer up better for Sunday. Lots of love from yours ever Ernest. PS hope you are in the best of health it is grand weather here today.'

PLATE 14 EASTBOURNE COLLEGE OTC MYTCHETT, AUGUST 1913

Even before war was declared, many young men from British public schools received military training, with weekly parades and a summer camp run for their school's Officers Training Corps (OTC). They were soon called to serve their country, although life expectancy was short. One who survived was Russell Llewellyn Mandeville Lloyd. Russell served in the King's Shropshire Light Infantry from 1914 to 1918 and finished the war as a Captain. He was wounded twice, mentioned in dispatches and awarded a Military Cross and Bar and the Croix de Guerre avec etoile. Russell sent a card home from his summer camp at Mytchett (just north of Aldershot) on 3 August 1913.

The Belgians have won for themselves the immortal glory which belongs to a people who prefer freedom to ease, and security even to life itself. We are all proud of their alliance and of their friendship. We salute them with respect and honour.

Extract from Mr Asquith's speech in the House of Commons. Aug 27 1914.

2 Propaganda

PLATE 16 THE GERMAN KAISER (EMPEROR) WILHELM II 1859–1941

ESPECIALLY DURING THE first two years of the war, postcards were used as part of a massive propaganda campaign. The first task was to inform the population that the war was just. On 3 August, the Germans declared war on France and the following day invaded Belgium after the Belgian authorities had denied German forces free passage through the country on their way to Paris. Subsequently, Britain declared war on Germany. This was a direct result of the London Treaty of 1830, guaranteeing Belgian neutrality, signed by both Britain and Germany (see plate 2).

PLATE 15 BRAVO BELGIUM

The card in the Valentine's Series was not postally used but quoted an extract from Herbert Asquith's speech in the House of Commons on 27 August 1914.

> 'The Belgians have won for themselves the immortal glory which belongs to a people who prefer freedom to ease, to security, even to life itself. We are proud of their alliance and their friendship. We salute them with respect and with honour.'

Donald McGill was quick to echo the Prime Minister's sentiments with a card posted on 6 November 1914 titled 'Hats Off! (to Belgium)'.

There was also a plan to portray the Germans as both evil and ridiculous, with the German Kaiser and his son 'Little Willie' singled out for ridicule.

This German card (above) was published in Berlin and sent to an address in that city in April 1915.

PLATE 17 THE CROWN PRINCE INSPECTING TROOPS

This very rare card shows Crown Prince Wilhelm, the Kaiser's son, inspecting troops. The card was not postally used. Dubbed 'Little Willie' by some, the Crown Prince was ridiculed on postcards as feckless and foppish.

PLATE 18 GOODBYE

'Dec 24 (1914) Brother Harry.

By the way do you see old Neddy stepping out I suppose he went faster than that when the old wiss bang was flying about "eh" Tom.'

PLATE 19 WANTED – GENERAL REPAIRS

The card was posted in Queenstown on 24 December 1914 to Miss K. Dinan. 'A very Happy Christmas 1914.'

Queenstown, in Ireland, is now known as Cobh. In April 1912, it had been the final port of call of the RMS Titanic just days before she struck an iceberg and sank.

PLATE 20 'AYE, AN' I'M THE SAFTEST O' THE FAMILY!'

The card drawn by Donald McGill in 1915 was sent to Mrs Sinclair, Kerr's Buildings, NewMill, Fife, Scotland.

> 'Jack Bruce is wounded again & in hospital at Le Harve he was only 4 days in the trenches I will write tomorrow and give you all the news as I am first going off to the Kirk Louis heard from the War Office last week hope you are both better Chris.'

PLATE 21 'ARMY MAKING SPLENDID PROGRESS' – EXTRACT FROM GERMAN WAR NEWS

The card was sent from Bovington Camp on 14 December 1914 to Mr J. Cottam, Carlton Scroop, near Grantham, Lincolnshire.

'Dear J.
Just a PC to let you know F Smith will be home for Christmas if no alteration. I forgot to tell our folks in the letter, so will you say I've told you. We are getting on champion, only it's so Mucky here, we get a bit of football at times. Hope to see you all been well in January. Hope your people are all well & you too, as I am glad to say I'm A1, so with best wishes from your old pal Reg. PS if you see Bob Cant tell him there's more muck here than at Lulworth so long.'

Smith may have been referring to Lulworth Camp, situated a few miles south of Bovington Camp.

PLATE 22 KILL THAT FLY

This Bamforth card in the War Cartoons series was posted in Barrow-in-Furness on 25 October 1914 to Miss A. Smith, 59 Clay Street, Workington, Cumberland. The writer asks, 'guess the sender'.

French, British, Belgian and Russian soldiers are depicted swatting a fly, which represents the Kaiser.

PLATE 23 HE WON'T BE HAPPY TILL HE GETS IT

The card was sent from London on 17 September 1914 to Mr J. Andrews, 8 Mill Street, Colchester, Essex. The message reads 'Do you know it won't come off.'

PLATE 24 WHICH IS THE QUICKEST WAY TO THE HOSPITAL?

An interesting card not only because it shows that the Kaiser had few fans in Britain, but because of the message on the back. What was in the cart? The card, printed and published by J Salmon, Sevenoaks, England, was sent from Bedford on 19 August 1917 to Master V Webb, 197 Dunstable Road, Luton, Beds (wellaired).

'Dear Vic
Just a card to let you know I'm having a fine time, I went round with the cart with Reggie this afternoon.
Love and Kisses Winkle'

PLATE 25 'FOR GOODNESS SAKE HALT! HERE KOM DOSE DEVILS, DER' – LINCOLNSHIRE YEOMANRY

The card, one of a series produced by J. Salmon and E. Mac, set out to show Germans as buffoons. They were overprinted with many different captions. This card has also been seen with the caption 'For gootness sake go back Here come der ROYAL ENGINEERS' and another 'Here come der CLIPSTONE BOYS.'

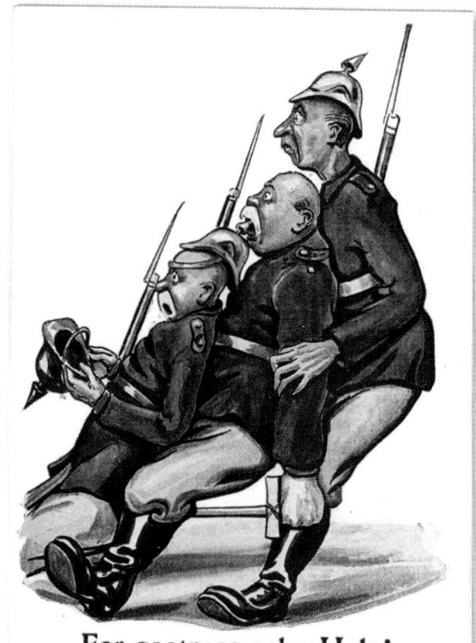

PLATE 26
KITCHENER'S MOTTO

It would seem that the Kaiser was in for a hard time and that the members of the British Empire would be joining the fight. The card was not postally used.

PLATE 27 HURRAH FOR THE ROYAL BERKS.!

Similarly, this card has also been seen with the caption 'Hurrah for the 11th YORKS.' Neither this card nor the one seen opposite were postally used.

The Kaiser's Arrival in Hell.

A Meeting was called of those who do dwell.
Down in the innermost depths of Hell,
The Chairman was one who is known to be pious—
He goes by the Name of Old Annanias

There were murderers, thieves and Whitaker Wright's
And the Devil was there to stop any fights,
A number of Germans arrived very late,
But quite soon enough to boast of their fate.

The Meeting was called to elect the best liar
To the onerous duties of tending the fire.
A motion was put to elect Mr. Crippen,
Who would give his attention to catching the dripping.,

The Kaiser then rose and recounted the deeds.
Of his cunning and treachery, while fighting round Liege
The faces of all went suddenly white,
When they heard of the fate of Louvain on that terrible night.

Lifting up his withered arm, and pointing to the sky,
He cursed and swore that it came from his English mothers side
To exterminate the British was my great wild desire,
As they stand in my way to be the world's sire.

Then old Ugly Krupp got up on his feet,
And denied Ananias such stories to beat,
But the Chairman replied that he had no desire,
For he thought the Kaiser should look after the fire.

The Meeting then voted that all of these crimes,
Commited by the Kaiser and his barbarous tribes,
Deserving recognition at the hands of Old Nick,
For the way they had worked the Confidence Trick.

So the Kaiser from Germany got the job on the spot,
For the lies that he told beat the whole blooming lot,
Even old Ananias was bound to admit,
He's proven his claim to the Bottomless Pit.

PLATE 28 THE KAISER'S ARRIVAL IN HELL

Some cards did not rely on illustrations to make a statement. No publisher is indicated on the back of the card, which was not postally used. German atrocities are listed in Liège and Louvain.

TEN LIDDLE GERMANS

TEN LIDDLE GERMANS
CAME ACROSS THE RHINE
ONE MET A BRITISHER
THEN THERE WERE NINE.

NINE LIDDLE GERMANS
WAR BREAD DID BAKE
ONE ATE A MOUTHFUL
THEN THERE WERE EIGHT.

EIGHT LIDDLE GERMANS
GAZED UP TO HEAVEN
ONE STOPPED A BULLET
THEN THERE WERE SEVEN.

SEVEN LIDDLE GERMANS
MUCHEE WINE MIX
ONE MET A GHURKA
THEN THERE WERE SIX.

SIX LIDDLE GERMANS
MOTOR CAR DRIVE
ARMED CAR CAME A BUST
THEN THERE WERE FIVE.

FIVE LIDDLE GERMANS
TRIED TO REACH THE SHORE
LIGHT CRUISER DROPPED SHELL
THEN THERE WERE FOUR.

FOUR LIDDLE GERMANS
TURNED ROUND TO FLEE
BARBED WIRE IN THE WAY
THEN THERE WERE THREE.

THREE LIDDLE GERMANS
MAKING DINNER STEW
SHRAPNEL STRUCK POT
THEN THERE WERE TWO.

TWO LIDDLE GERMANS
LOOKING VERY GLUM
ONE MET A BAYONET
THEN THERE WAS ONE.

ONE LIDDLE GERMAN
WORN OUT AND DONE
TURNED UP HIS TOES
THEN THERE WAS NONE.

ONE FRANTIC KAISER TEARING AT HIS HAIR
"WHERE ARE MY SOLDIERS ?" ECHO ANSWERS—"WHERE ?" G.H.L.

PLATE 29 TEN LIDDLE GERMANS

The card, which was not postally used and was copyrighted E. Mack, King Henry's Road, Hampstead, London, may have echoed the nursery rhyme 'Ten Green Bottles'. A similar rhyme was used by Agatha Christie in her play *And Then There Were None,* first published in November 1939.

PLATE 30 'NATIONS REMEMBER! HERE THE VICTIMS ... THERE THE MURDERER!!' – GERMAN ATROCITIES

PLATE 30

The card, published in Paris in 1917, lists many German atrocities, including the sinking of the *Lusitania* by the German U-20, commanded by Captain Schweiger, on 7 May 1915. Lusitania took only 18 minutes to sink, with the loss of 1,198 lives (although the card lists 1,150 fatalities).

The execution of Nurse Edith Cavell by the Germans on 12 October 1915 after she helped British soldiers caught behind enemy lines to escape proved a propaganda coup for the British, who reported her death as evidence of German war crimes. Edith Cavell's body lies in Norwich Cathedral.[3] The Kaiser is depicted trying to hide historical truth, held by a woman, from being proclaimed.[4]

Edith Cavell was executed by a firing squad and not as described on the back of this French card, which was not postally used.

> 'Condemned to death by a military tribunal in Belgium, under the charge of having favoured the evasion of British soldiers, Miss Edith Cavell, of Norwich, a voluntary nurse, is taken to the execution ground on the 12th of October at day break. She faints: the German officer gives his soldiers the order to fire, they hesitate to shoot on the prostrate body of a woman. The fiend takes his revolver and leaning upon his victim, deliberately blows her brains out. REMEMBER!'[5]

PLATE 31 'MISS EDITH CAVELL MURDERED OCTOBER 12TH 1915 REMEMBER!'

PLATE 32 THE GERMAN ARMY IS NOT BAD AT A 'PINCH'

The card sent from Manchester to Liverpool on 8 April 1915 was published by Inter-Art Co., Red Lion Square, London, which was run by Robert McCrumb. McCrumb was Donald McGill's publisher from 1914 to 1931.[6]

The German Army was accused of large-scale looting in Belgium, among other things.

PLATE 33 'KULTUR!!!'

PLATE 33

Taken from the *Daily Telegraph*, 7 October 1914:

> 'COMING OF THE VANDALS
> By GRANVILLE FORTESCUE
> "You who are sheltered from the grim realities of war remember the people of Belgium."'

On the back of the card it reads, 'If you cannot join the Army – join the Anti-German League.'

PLATE 34 BACK OF CARD

Taken from the *Daily Telegraph* of 20 July 1915:

> 'PERSONAL AN APPEAL TO THE NATION
> The ANTI-GERMAN LEAGUE, of 25 Victoria Street, Westminster makes the following URGENT APPEAL for FUNDS for the purpose of carrying out a huge Anti-German campaign throughout the country. … The Germans have committed crimes against all human forgiveness. From the ruined homesteads of stricken Belgium – from the blood-drenched plains of Northern France, their guilt cries aloud to Heaven for vengeance, and there can be no readmission for them to the free Commonwealth of Europe.'

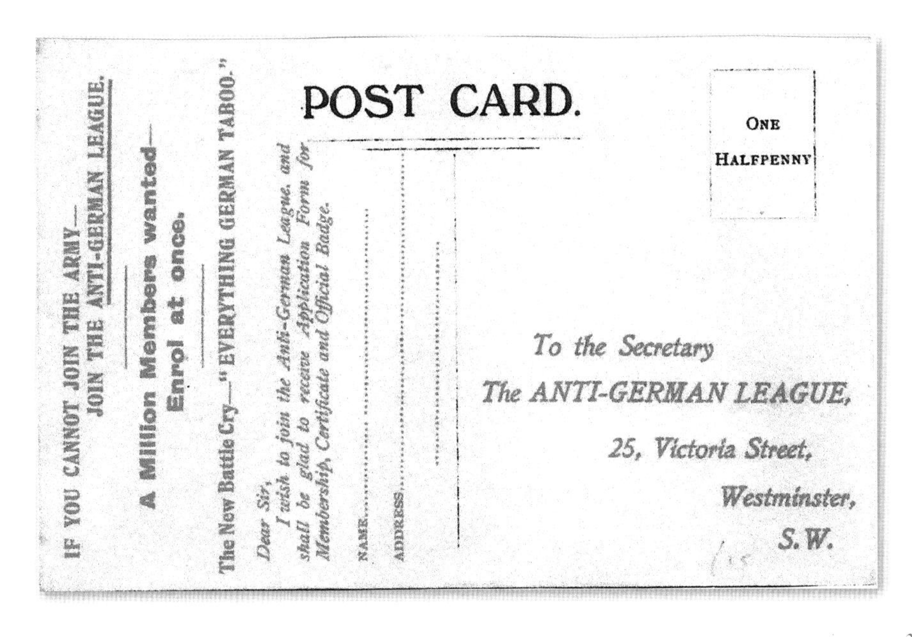

IF YOU CANNOT JOIN THE ARMY—
JOIN THE ANTI-GERMAN LEAGUE.

A Million Members wanted—
Enrol at once.

The New Battle Cry—"EVERYTHING GERMAN TABOO."

Dear Sir,
I wish to join the Anti-German League, and shall be glad to receive Application Form for Membership, Certificate and Official Badge.

NAME..

ADDRESS..

POST CARD.

ONE HALFPENNY

To the Secretary
The ANTI-GERMAN LEAGUE,
25, Victoria Street,
Westminster,
S.W.

The Flags that fight in Freedom's Cause

Great Britain and Ireland

France

Belgium

Russia

3 Flags

FLAGS WERE USED extensively on postcards to emphasise the solidarity of the Allied nations, even if the flag of Great Britain was on occasions portrayed as the flag of England.

PLATE 35 THE FLAGS THAT FIGHT IN FREEDOM'S CAUSE

This card in the Classic All British series was published by Will Sharpe Ltd, Bradford & London, and sent to Miss Elspeth Gilbertson, 16 Watergate, Grantham on 22 March 1915. The flags of Belgium and Russia have been added to those of Great Britain & Ireland and France.

> 'Many thanks for very nicely written letter. Are the cat, kittens and guinea pigs all in the same hutch. I think I shall be staying until Wednesday not later. Love from Mother.'

The card was posted in Earls Court, London.

PLATE 36 UNDER TWO FLAGS

The Donald McGill card was sent from Grahamstown, South Africa to an address in Cape Province. It shows Britain and France united.

PLATE 37 THE OLDEST ALLIES IN EUROPE 1295–1914 – FRANCE AND SCOTLAND UNITED

The card was sent from Edinburgh on 25 January 1916 to Master Billy Jones, 4 Bethia Cottages, New Road, Weybridge, Surrey.

> 'I have not forgotten your bicycle ride I promised you write soon.'

PLATE 38

John Bull, the personi-fication of England, is about to carve up Germany between the four Allies. On the back of the card, which was not dated or postally used, Len sends birthday wishes to his Uncle Alf.

PLATE 38 'NOW GENTS, WHICH PORTION AM I TO CARVE FOR YOU!'

PLATE 39 THE FLAGS OF THE ALLIES

The card, copyright E. Mack, King Henry's Road, Hampstead, London, was printed and published by J. Salmon, Sevenoaks, England. It was posted from Richmond, Surrey on 31 July 1915 to Miss Beswick, Rose Cottage, Balsham, Cambs.

'Hope you arrived allright M.'

The flags of Serbia, Japan and Italy have been added.

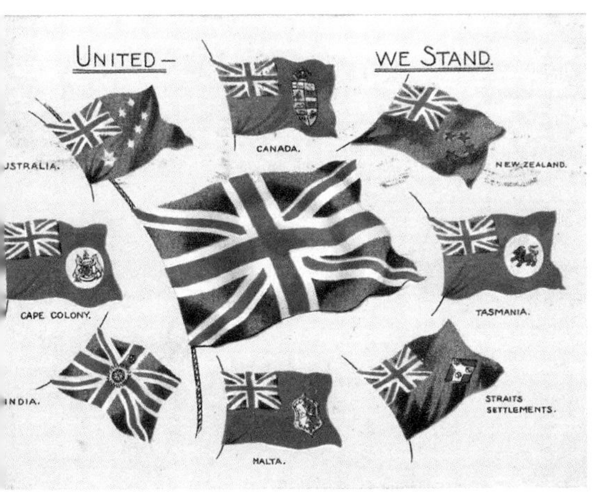

PLATE 40 UNITED WE STAND

The card, another in the All British series, shows the flag of Great Britain surrounded by those of her colonies. The flags of Australia, New Zealand, Canada and India are joined by those of Malta, Tasmania (Australia), Cape Colony and Straits Settlements (South Africa). Hundreds of thousands of soldiers from the colonies fought for the Allied cause, ensuring that what had been a European conflict became a worldwide one.

The card was sent from Paddington, London on 28 April 1915 to Mr J.H. Pinches, Roslyn Villa, Wotherton, Chirbury, Salop.

'Dear Jay I saw this card yesterday and thought you would like it. Love to all I. P.'

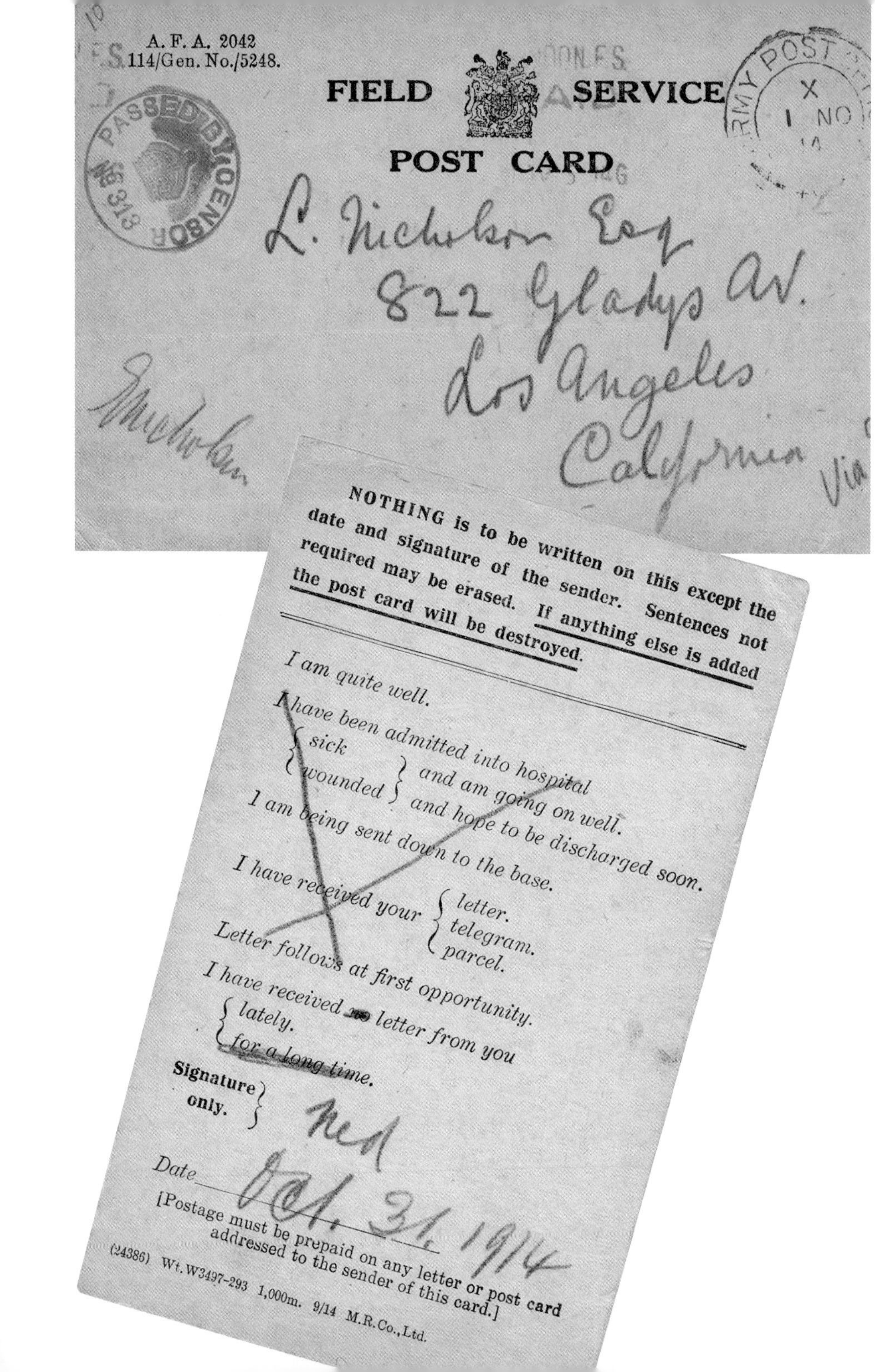

A. F. A. 2042
114/Gen. No./5248.

FIELD SERVICE

POST CARD

PASSED BY CENSOR
No 313

ARMY POST OFFICE
X
1 NO
14

L. Nicholson Esq
822 Gladys Av.
Los Angeles
California
Via

Nicholson

NOTHING is to be written on this except the date and signature of the sender. Sentences not required may be erased. If anything else is added the post card will be destroyed.

I am quite well.

I have been admitted into hospital
{ sick } and am going on well.
{ wounded } and hope to be discharged soon.

I am being sent down to the base.

I have received your { letter. telegram. parcel.

Letter follows at first opportunity.

I have received no letter from you
{ lately.
{ for a long time.

Signature only. Ned

Date Oct. 31. 1914

[Postage must be prepaid on any letter or post card addressed to the sender of this card.]

(24386) Wt. W3497–293 1,000m. 9/14 M.R.Co.,Ltd.

4 Cards and Letters Home and the Censor

Both when in training or at the front, soldiers and sailors sent letters to, and hoped to receive letters from, their families and loved ones. Many messages were sent as letters, some as postcards, and some as postcards enclosed in envelopes. No stamps were required on letters or cards sent by those on active service. All mail sent from the front had to be passed by the censor, usually a junior officer. A blue pencil was used to strike through offending passages, including the location from which the card or letter was sent. The original censor stamps taken with the British Expeditionary Force in August 1914 and used until December of that year were small, red, circular hand stamps.

Examples of stamped censor marks used throughout the war can be seen on page 170.

PLATE 41 FIELD SERVICE POSTCARDS

The card, written 31 October 1914 and posted the next day, was sent by 'Ned' to L. Nicholson Esq, 822 Gladys Avenue, Los Angeles, California (via England). The field service postcard was a means of getting a simple message home without having to go to the trouble of writing a letter.

PLATE 42 BACK OF FIELD SERVICE POSTCARD

The field service postcard was completed by crossing out the prepared sentences, apart from the soldier's name and the date of posting. If anything else was added, the postcard would often have been destroyed.

> 'I am quite well. I have received a letter from you lately. Ned 31 Oct. 1914.'

PLATE 43 LA NOUVELLE POSTE, BOULOGNE-SUR-MER – L.L.

This French card, posted on 25 November 1914, would have been bought locally in a shop in the base camp or rear area. It shows the new post office in the town. The 'L.L.' indicates that the card was published by Levy Sons & Co. of Paris.

George writes to his sister:

> 'Dear Sister Many thanks for such a nice parcel it is so good of you. A letter is following the PC. Love to all news in letter from loving brother George xxx.'

Silver war badge (see page 53).

PLATE 44 EN GUERRE – MITRAILLEUSES BELGES

Sent to Miss D. Fairclough, 60 W Stockwell Street, Colchester, England. This Belgian card was posted on 3 April 1915 and the card shows a machine gun pulled by dogs.

From December 1914 to April 1915 the censor marks for the Western Front changed to a square. A square censor mark was also used in the Middle East.

Mary box (see page 79).

PLATE 45 RUE DU COMMERCE, PORT SAID

The card was posted on 14 August 1915 to Mrs Askew, 81 Queens Road, East Grinstead, Sussex, England. There is a square censor mark on the back of the card.

> 'My own dearest wife Doll. Just a few more lines hoping you are well and getting on alright these are a few PC's where we are now have been here a few days but shall soon be moving again pleased to say I am well I'm waiting to hear from mine soon.'

The censor has signed the card 'R Loder'.

PLATE 46 GLOIRE AU 75

This card with a triangle censor mark was posted on 4 July 1915. 'Ned' writes to Mrs Brand (his wife), Keith Hall, Inverurie, Aberdeenshire, Scotland.

> 'Dear Jeannie,
> We are in a fine grassy orchard well back from the line resting, bathing and eating cherries & some getting furlough hope I may get a run home before we go back to the line. Ned.'

The French card, printed in Paris, celebrates the 75mm field gun, said to be the best of the war. It was one of the first field guns to feature a system of recuperation, which virtually eliminated recoil when the gun was fired, hence doing away with the need to re-aim after each round. This gave the gun a remarkable rate of fire.[7,8]

The hexagon censor mark was used on the Western Front from 4 January 1916 to 7 November 1916.

A triangle was used as a censor mark on the Western Front from April 1915 to 4 January 1916, as well as in Salonika and the Middle East from April 1916 to October 1917. A card posted on 20 April 1915 received both a square and a triangular censor mark.

PLATE 47 THE QUAY TOWARDS THE RESERVOIR

The card was posted on 4 September 1916 from the front, rather than from the town of Le Tréport.

> 'Dear Ede,
> Just a card to wish you many happy returns of the 6th. This is one of the cards left from my recent "holiday" of which I shall retain many jolly memories. Should like to be running over for another game of ping pong – it's a quieter game than the one we're accustomed to play out here. Old Fritz has a knack of "feuding" with the sort of balls that hurt when they hit. You ought to see the – up on yonder ridge as I write. No – with fondest regards yours, Les.'

Les may have been in hospital in or near Le Tréport but had returned to the front by the time he wrote the postcard.

An oval censor mark was used on the Western Front from 7 November 1916 to October 1917.

PLATE 48 LA PLACE DE LA REPUBLIQUE, LE MANS

A card, posted on 12 October 1917, features La Place de la Republique in Le Mans. Oliver writes to his parents in Leeds:

> 'Dear M&F Just a line to let you know I am quite well & still – I am at the 2nd Rest Camp somewhere in France and having a splendid time. I've spent 2 days & 2 nights in the – so far plenty to eat & plenty of rain Seen hundreds of apple trees and vines and lovely scenery. Oliver.'

An octagon was the censor mark for Salonika from September 1917 and was also used in other parts of the Middle East.

The sensor mark on the Western Front from October 1917 to 1919 (and also in Italy) was a rectangle. On 5 April 1918, George writes to Miss F. Potter, 130 Rookery Road, Handsworth, Birmingham.

> 'Dear Miss Potter,
> Many thanks for your most welcome letter which I was very pleased to receive. I'm sorry I've not been able to answer your letter before now. I trust you will excuse me. Owing to the conditions of affairs out here at present, there's no such luck as having time to ourselves. Trusting this PC finds all at home in the best of health. Yours truly George.'

Could Miss Potter have been a former teacher, a family friend or one of the many women who sent letters and sometimes socks to the troops at the front?

PLATE 49 LA GRANDE GUERRE 1914–15 – BATTERIE D'ARTILLERIE FRANÇAISE DE 75EN ACTION SUR LE FRONT AUX ENVIRONS D'ARRAS

The card depicts a French battery of 75mm field guns in action near Arras. The card was printed in 1915, three years before it was used.

PLATE 50 THE CITADEL, CAIRO

On a card posted in December 1918, 'Will' wishes Miss Gwen Mayhew of 18 Constable Road, Felixstowe, England 'A very Happy Xmas and a prosperous New Year'.

PLATE 51 BUON NATALE – MERRY CHRISTMAS TO YOU

On this card, posted on 17 December 1918 and sent to Mrs M. Small, 5 Clifton Mansions, Coldharbour Lane, Brixton, London, Mr Small writes:

> 'Dear Wife, just to wish you a happy Xmas & trust I shall be with you early in the New Year.'

A shield censor mark was used in Italy from 1918.

PLATE 52 AT AUBERVILLIERS STATION

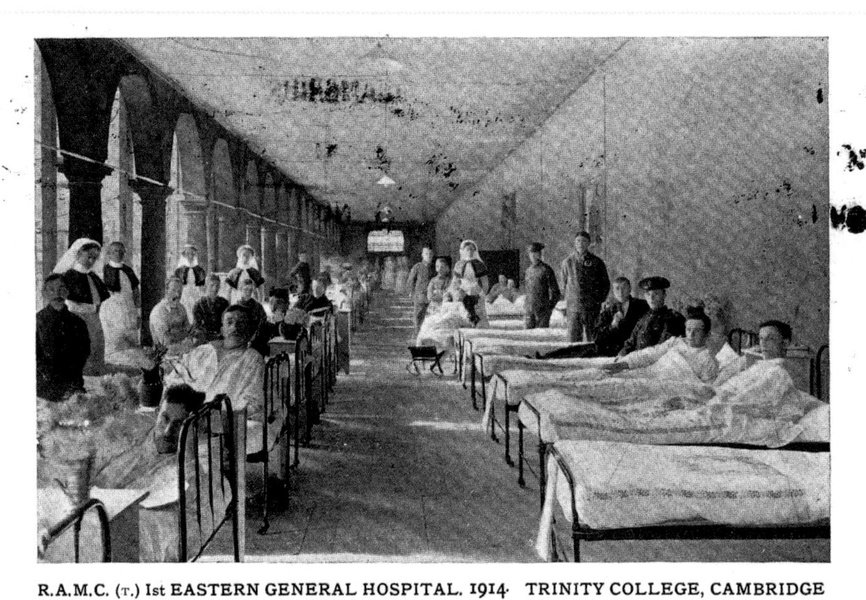

PLATE 53 RAMC (T) 1ST EASTERN GENERAL HOSPITAL – 1914

5 Blue Boys

THE WAR WOULD not be over by Christmas. Few had foreseen the effect of the new weapons that were to be used in the conflict. The newly perfected machine gun, with a firing speed of 600 rounds per minute, along with the use of artillery and poison gas produced an horrific number of casualties. The conditions in the trenches, often rat-infested and on occasions flooded, led at best to uncomfortable living and at worst to illness or even death. From the earliest days of the war, wounded soldiers arrived back in Britain bound for military hospitals and then military convalescent camps.

PLATE 52

A card sent to Phyllis Howes, 27 Fellowes Place, Stoke, Devonport, Devon on 17 February 1915 shows a team preparing a meal for wounded soldiers who were being evacuated by train from the front. Aubervilliers Station is on the north side of Paris.

PLATE 53

The card, sent to Miss Connie Reeves, c/o Gill S., Bridge House, Dartford, Kent on 6 November 1914, shows a ward at Trinity College, Cambridge, which had been requisitioned for use by the Royal Army Medical Corps (RAMC) to treat some of the early casualties of the war.

Will writes:

> 'Dearest Connie Received your letter this dinnertime liked it a lot. It has been an awful afternoon here had a big thunderstorm absolutely pouring with rain Will write you a letter tomorrow no more news at present yours with Love etc Will xxx'

One of the first priorities was to replace khaki uniforms, which in many cases were dirty, worn out and infested with lice. The soldiers were therefore issued with a uniform known as 'Convalescent Blues', which consisted of blue trousers and tunics with a white shirt and red tie, worn with a khaki service dress cap or other headdress appropriate to the regiment or nationality of the soldier. Wearers were therefore known as the 'Blue Boys'. To save on costs, the uniform was produced in only a few sizes and generally fitted very badly. If the trousers were too long, they were turned up, as faithfully drawn by cartoonist Donald McGill and others.

PLATE 54 'I WONDER IF KISSES IS BAD FOR WOUNDS?'

As early as October 1915, McGill's cards were available on the Western Front, with captions written in both English and French, even if much was often lost in translation. They were used by both English and French-speaking troops, as well as the Belgians.

According to Dr Anna Carden-Coyne, 'In hospitals and convalescent homes, flirtations, fantasies, romance and intimate bonding captivated both patients and staff, especially at Christmas time. Indeed many women met their future husbands in the wards.'[9]

Joseph Pownall of Preston, Lancashire served in the Lancashire Fusiliers. He was wounded in France in 1917 and evacuated back to England and then sent to Summerdown Convalescent Camp in Eastbourne. While there he met a local girl, Frances Pullon, who he married towards the end of the war. After the war Joseph worked for the Eastbourne Waterworks Company. He and his wife lived in a company cottage where they raised eleven children.

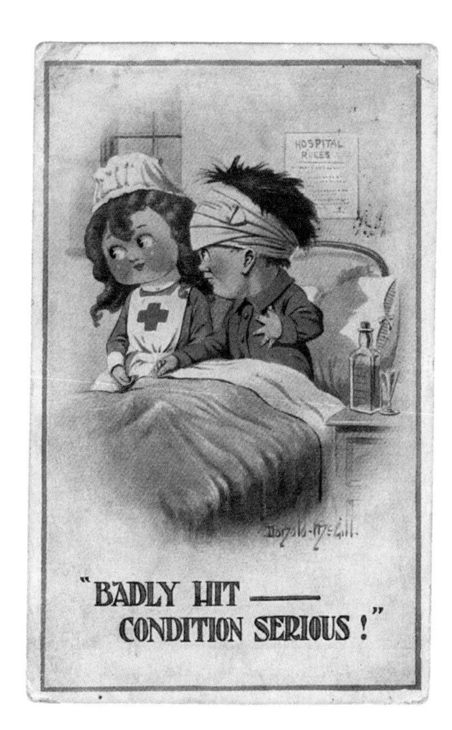

PLATE 55 'BADLY HIT – CONDITION SERIOUS!'

On a card, posted from Margate on 28 July 1916, McGill illustrated this intimate bonding. The nurse and the patient are not only holding hands but would seem to be sharing a bed. Are they breaking hospital rules?

PLATE 56 'IS BLUE YOUR FAVOURITE COLOUR? I SEE GIRLS GO IN FOR IT A LOT NOW-A-DAYS!'

This Bamforth card was sent from Walsall on 26 September 1918 to Miss F. Sharp, 7 Cliff Street, Padiham, Lancs.

> 'Nice colour just now. Don't you think so? £0÷2'

Could it be that the writer had no money and was suggesting dividing the absent money with Miss Sharp?

The sentiments expressed in the card shown in plate 11 ('Keep a heart that's true') showed the fears of those serving at the front that troops on leave, those serving on the home front (including special constables), or even Blue Boys might steal away their loved ones.

The card showing the view of Summerdown Camp as seen from the junction of Paradise Drive and Summerdown Road was sent by Jack on 24 March 1918 to Miss E. Harvey, Dicq Road, St Luke's, Jersey.

> 'My darling Just arrived at this place & it is fine. We are quite close to the beach & as the weather is glorious it is tophole. I am getting on fine but my arm is still painful. However bless just look what I am missing. The Germans have started their great push just where I was. I hope to be home soon and it will be lovely as weather is coming on. Write soon Dear yours for Ever Jack.'[10]

The 'great push' was the Ludendorff offensive, which began on 21 March 1918. Led by the eponymous general, it targeted the lightly held British front on the old Somme battlefield, perhaps the weakest point in the Allies' line. The casualty list of men killed or wounded was immense, with the Germans losing 348,000, the French 112,000 and the British 343,000.

On Friday 3 November 1916, King George V and Queen Mary visited the camp. It was reported that they were able to see the Massage Institute, the Sick Lines (where the men slept), 'Park Lane' (some artistically painted huts), 'C' lines and the Quartermaster's Stores.[11]

PLATE 57 SUMMERDOWN CAMP

PLATE 58 'PARK LANE'

'Park Lane' was a nickname given to 'A' lines, a row of convalescent huts looking south towards Beresford House, a private girls school, which closed in 1991. The card, which was not postally used, was produced by Compton's, 32/34 High Street, Eastbourne.

Another card produced by Compton's Photographer, High Street, Old Town, Eastbourne was sent on 8 October 1915 to Mr and Mrs J. Shoday, Leytonstone, London. It depicts camp staff and Blue Boys outside one of the 'artistically painted' huts in 'C' lines. Gardening seems to have been popular and much that did not move was painted white.[12]

The military authorities realised that recreation was an important part of a soldier's physical and mental recovery. Gardening was popular, as was football. There was a gymnasium at Summerdown Camp, which doubled as a theatre and was also used to show films. There was also a skittle alley, a room for playing billiards, and a room set apart for letter writing. The soldiers were allowed into the town after 1 p.m. and the Blue Boys often went bathing in the sea or took out a rowing boat.[13]

PLATE 59 'C' LINES AT SUMMERDOWN CAMP

PLATE 60 THE BILLIARD ROOM

It may well be that the Blue Boys billeted at Summerdown Camp were not downhearted.

PLATE 61 'ARE WE DOWNHEARTED? NO!'

Many war songs were promoted on postcards. Examples include 'Are we downhearted? No!' This upbeat verse, often belted out by a platoon of marching soldiers, became one of the most popular rallying cries during the war.

'Are we downhearted? No!

Then let your voices ring

And altogether sing

Are we downhearted? No!'

PLATE 62 I THINK YOU CALLED?

During the early years of the war, large numbers of Indian soldiers enlisted to help the mother country in her hour of need. An Indian soldier resplendent in his turban is featured on a McGill postcard postally used on 23 May 1915.

From 1914 to 1916 many of those who were wounded were treated in Brighton in the Royal Pavilion and the Dome. Running the military hospital was an administrative nightmare because of the differences in religion and caste. Patients were grouped together according to tribe and caste, and every ward had two taps – one for Hindus and one for Muslims.

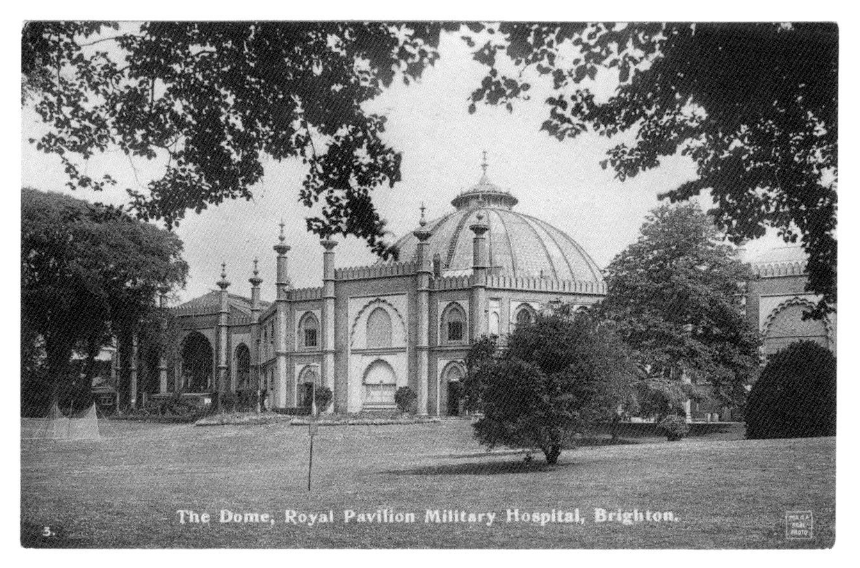

PLATE 63 THE DOME, ROYAL PAVILION MILITARY HOSPITAL, BRIGHTON
These cards were printed for sale in the hospital. Card not postally used.

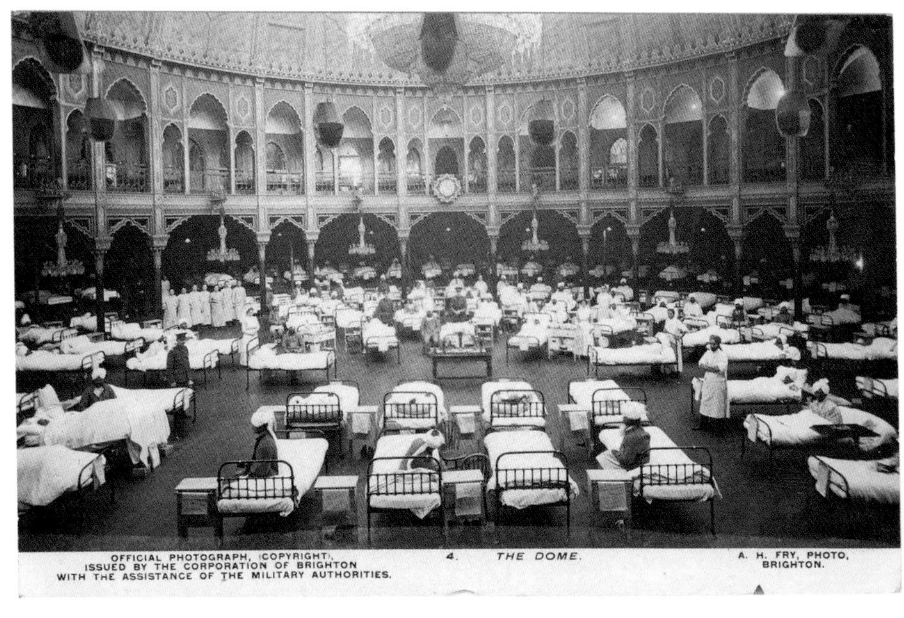

PLATE 64 THE DOME, ROYAL PAVILION, BRIGHTON

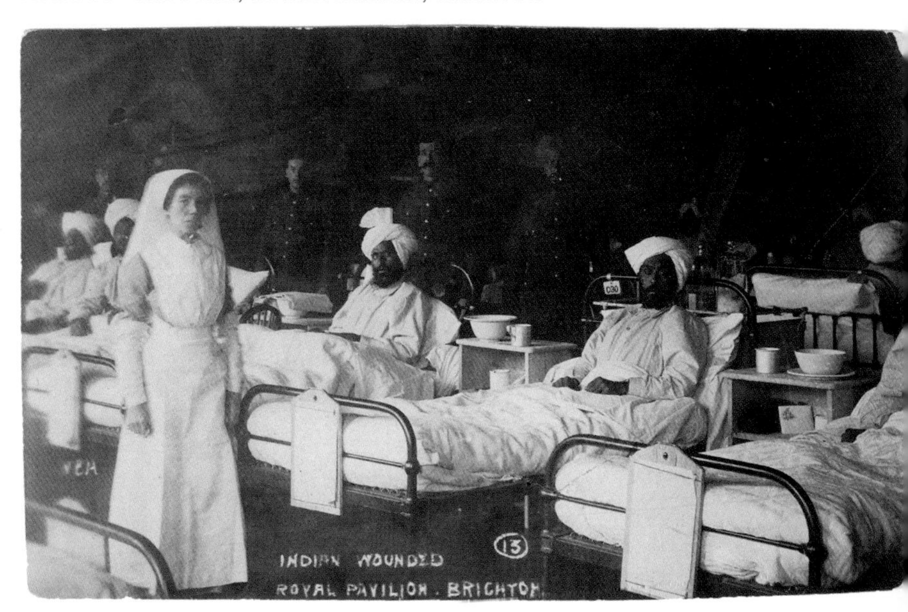

PLATE 65 INDIAN WOUNDED AT ROYAL PAVILION, BRIGHTON

Alfred Lifton enlisted in 1914. Like many young soldiers, Private Lifton had his photograph taken in his new army uniform. In this case, Alfred posed with a friend, possibly Miss Doris Foster. In 1915 Lifton went to France with the 1st Cambridgeshire Regiment, 18th Brigade within the 39th Division. It may well be that, at that time, knowing he might be killed in action, Alfred wrote on the back of the card, 'If found will the finder kindly return it to Miss Doris Foster, 4 Cavour Road, Sheerness, Kent, England – Private Lifton 327212 D Coy. 16 Platoon, 1 Cambridgeshire Reg 118th Brigade 39th Division France'. The card may well have been kept in the breast pocket of his uniform.

Alfred was wounded in the Ypres salient in April 1917 and evacuated back to Britain. In May of the same year he was treated in Ward B3 of Moseley Road Hospital, Fallowfield, Manchester. Alfred Lifton, now a Lance Corporal, was finally discharged as physically unfit for further active service on 3 September 1919. Lifton was awarded the British War Medal (1914–18), the Victory Medal and the Silver War Badge. The latter was awarded as a lapel badge for wounded soldiers when recuperating in order to denote that they had served, avoiding derision and white feathers. The card was not postally used.

PLATE 66 PRIVATE ALFRED LIFTON 327212

PLATE 67 HOUSES BOMBARDED BY THE GERMANS AT CREIL

PLATE 68 LA GRANDE GUERRE 1914–15: LILLE – ASPECT DE LA RUE FAIDHERBE APRÈS LA BOMBARDMENT

6 Cards from Somewhere in France – 1915

Having crossed into France, soldiers used the cards that were available locally. Some cards showed scenes taken before the start of hostilities and some showed the destruction caused by bombardments.

PLATE 67

The card, posted on 9 February 1915 to Mary in New York, USA, shows damage to buildings in Creil, a town north of Paris. What is unusual is that the card was posted in Edinburgh and not in France. The card may well have been sold in Edinburgh having been produced by 'William Ritchie and Sons Ltd, Edinburgh and London – sole agents for the United Kingdom and British colonies.'

'Dear Mary
You might let me know if Bella is living or dead I have not had a postcard from her for a very long time now she was to send me lots of cards but I think that somebody else is getting them all PS Robert expects to be at the Front very soon.'

PLATE 68

A card posted on 15 April 1915 shows the Rue Faidherbe in Lille after a bombardment. Not only is there damage to buildings but a large number of horses or mules have perished.

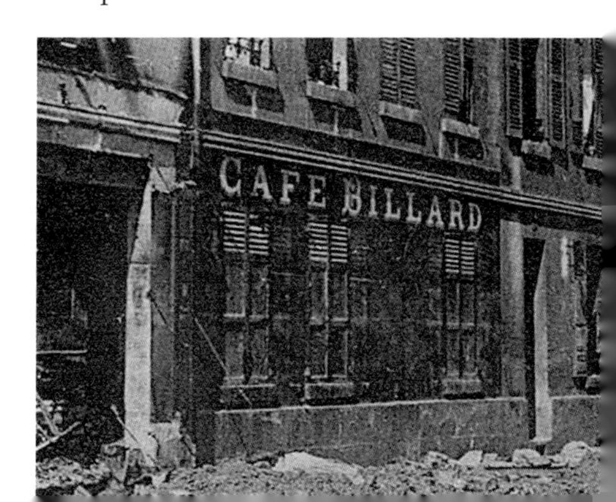

PLATE 69 AUTHIE (SOMME) – VUE PARTIELLE

The card, showing a partial view of the village of Authie, located in France near the border with Belgium and north-east of Amiens, has been 'lightly' censored. The village church is on the right of the photograph and a large cross stands next to the road in the centre of the picture.

On the back, Ernest wrote to his mother on 22 October 1915:

> 'Dearest Mother
> Just to let you know I am well and as usual excepting for being cold. I used to live in this pretty village. Luckily the Germans did very little damage when they went through
> Tons of love Ernest.'

PLATE 70 LAVENTIE – VUE D'ENSEMBLE

The card, posted on 3 December 1915 and lightly censored, was sent to Miss V. Thompson, VAD Hospital, 2 Church Road, Ashford, Kent.

> 'Darling
> Many thanks for 2 letters the Photos were ripping. Have just moved again Goodbye Fondest love Frank'

Laventie was a small farming and light industrial town situated just west of Lille. The town was heavily fought over between German and Allied forces. From 1915 there was constant underground fighting in the area.

PLATE 71 A KISS FROM FRANCE

PLATE 72 FORGET ME NOT

7 Silk Poscards

By far the most cherished postcards sent from the front were silk postcards. From early 1915 they were produced in large numbers as part of a cottage industry, located in northern France, which saw mainly women engaged in intricate designs that were hand-embroidered on to strips of silk mesh. These strips were then sent to factories for cutting and mounting as postcards and greeting cards. It is estimated that about 10 million were produced.[14]

PLATE 73 SOUVENIR OF ROUEN

This superior silk postcard depicts the Paschal Lamb (the coat of arms of the city of Rouen), the symbol of St John (the patron saint of Rouen), and six flags of the Allies. There is no writing on the back of the card, which would have been sent in an envelope or hand-delivered when the soldier was home on leave.

PLATE 74 ROYAL ENGINEERS

PLATE 75 HAND-PAINTED CARD – FORGET ME NOT

Hand-painted cards were also available and less expensive than silks. On the back of the card, featuring five flags of the Allies and clover, 'Daddy' has written:

> 'Nov 5 1915 Somewhere in France with love to Harry xxxx From Daddy.'

Unfortunately, the father has written his message on both sides of the card. A similar hand-painted card, written on the same day, was sent to Harry's brother, Willie. The card states:

> 'My Bearts Right to Bere!'

This should be 'My Heart's Right Here!' (h has been written as b). Spelling errors are often found on these cards. No wonder that by the time the artists were nearing the end of the umpteenth version of some design, especially if they were not English speakers, errors occurred.

Forget · me · not ·
Love
From Daddy
Nov 5th 1915
Somewhere
in France

PLATE 76 LE RÊVE ('THE DREAM')

In Memorium.

"Called to Higher Service, June 5th, 1916."

Oh ! Gallant Life so freely given,
Brave Heart in death for ever stilled.
In ocean's arms you quietly sleep
Your glorious destiny fulfilled.
Hero—who died for honour's sake,
Our tears, our prayers, our homage take.

PLATE 77 'IN MEMORIAM – CALLED TO HIGHER SERVICE, JUNE 5TH 1916'

The card, not postally used, commemorates the death of Lord Kitchener as a result of the sinking of HMS *Hampshire* on 5 June 1916.

8 Cards from Somewhere in France – 1916

PLATE 76

'Ned' sent a sentimental card to his wife Jeannie, 11 months after one sent on 4 July 1915 (plate 46).

> 'My dear Jeannie 9/6/16 sorry to hear that the weather is so wet but it may get better soon, bad job about D off K but I suppose he'll be easier replaced than if it had been his army as long as we have a lot of braves with conscience enough to look after home we'll come through alright. I'm getting on great & would have been fine pleased if I had a visit home before going back. best love to all x Ned.'

PLATE 78 LA CATHÉDRALE ET LE MARCHÉ SUR L'EAU, AMIENS – L.L.

PLATE 78

The card, posted on 8 July 1916, shows the cathedral at Amiens. The censor has erased the name of the city and the waterside market. The card was sent to Mrs Coe, Butchers Arms, London Road, Beccles, Suffolk.

> 'Dear Mother just a line to let you know I am getting on alright Love from Bert xxxx.'

The Butchers Arms still stands on the London Road in Beccles.

PLATE 79 BOUQUE-MAISON (SOMME)

The censor has removed the area of the card showing the location of this rural village. In fact, the card shows the Rue de Doullon in Bouque-Maison (Somme), located north of Amiens on the border between France and Belgium. On 28 August 1916, a father wrote to his daughter, Irene:

> 'My dear Daughter Hope you are well with love from Dad.'

PLATE 80 ROUEN PLACE CARNOT – VIEW OF THE QUAYS AND THE BOLELDIEN BRIDGE

The card was sent on 6 November 1916 to Miss M. Hadfield, 34 Park Street, Shifnal (just east of Telford), Shropshire by Private H. Felton, 60659 RAMC, no 10 General Hospital, BEF Rouen.

> 'Not a Patient this time on Duty.'

The censor has blanked out the location, which was written in both French and English.

PLATE 81 THEY DON'T CARE ABOUT THE GRAPESHOT

Sentimental French cards were available in large numbers and eagerly collected in albums. This card was posted on 2 July 1916 and sent to Miss A. Spearing, Paradise Mills, Langport, Somerset.

> 'Dear Ada
> just a card to add to your album hoping you are in the best of health as it leaves me A1 with kind regards to you all & Dad & Ma. From uncle Fred.'

The following was written in French to accompany the message:

> 'They don't care about the grapeshot,
> It's the country that awaits them
> We can win the battle
> When it's France that we defend.'

PLATE 82 FOOTBALL KICKED OFF BY CAPTAIN WILFRED P. NEVILL

Wilfred Nevill was born in London on 14 July 1894. He was educated at Dover College, where he was head prefect as well as captain of the cricket and hockey teams. He also played in the 1st XV for the rugby team. Nevill went up to Jesus College, Cambridge in 1913 to study the classical Tripos. While there, he became a member of the University Officer Training Corps (O.T.C.) and attended the 1914 summer training camp at Mytchett, just north of Aldershot.

Nevill enlisted in November 1914, and by July 1916 he was a captain attached to the East Surrey Regiment. He became famous as the officer who kicked a football into no man's land at the start of the Battle of the Somme. He was promptly killed in action while leading an assault on a German position.

Writing to Nevill's mother, Major Irwin paid this tribute:

> 'He was one of the bravest men I have ever met, and was loved and trusted by his men to such a degree they would have followed him anywhere.' (Major A.P.B. Irwin, Billie, The Nevill Letters, 1914–16)

One of the footballs Nevill kicked into the battlefield at the Somme is currently displayed at the Princess of Wales Royal Regiment Museum in Dover.

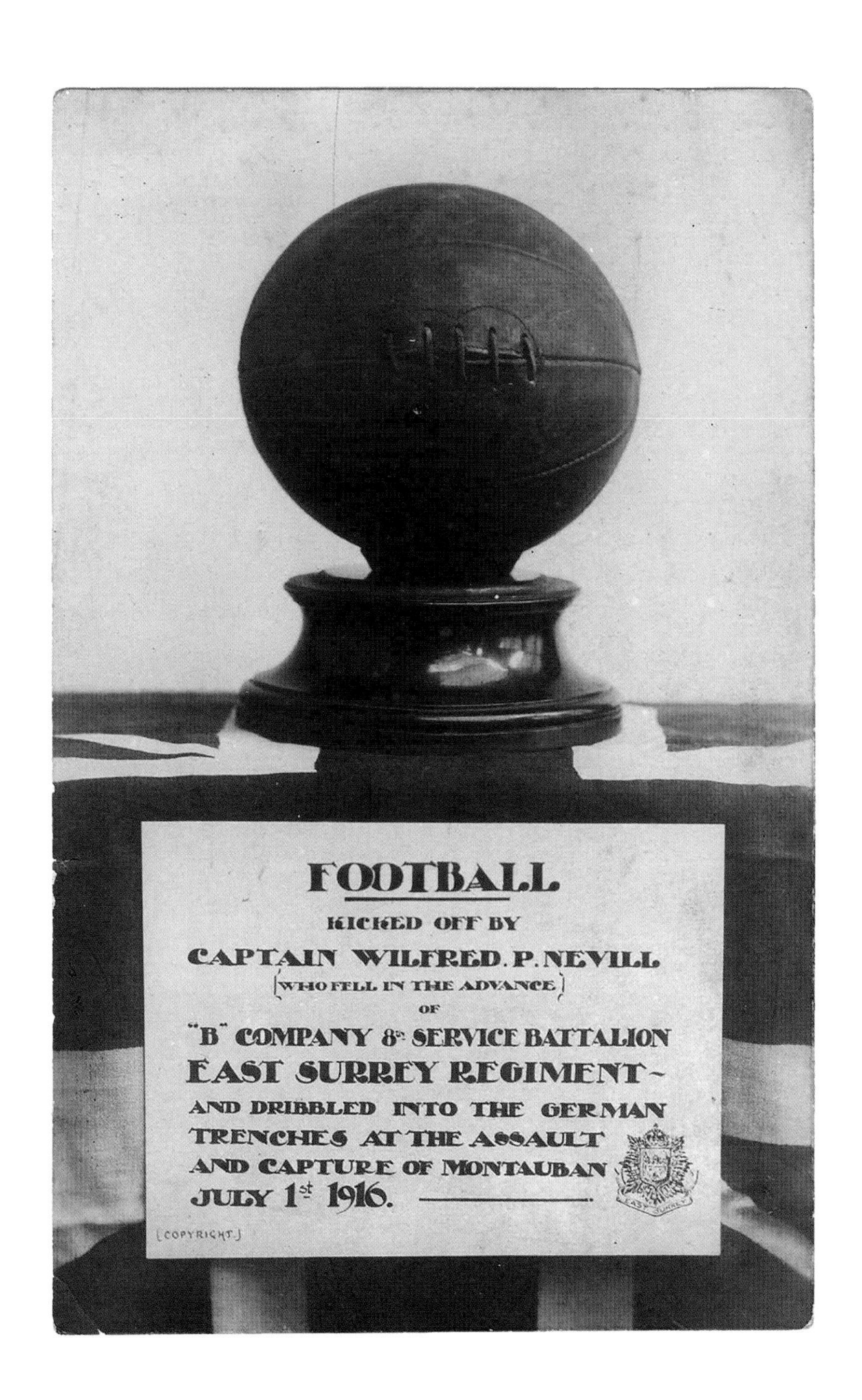
FOOTBALL
KICKED OFF BY
CAPTAIN WILFRED. P. NEVILL
(WHO FELL IN THE ADVANCE)
OF
"B" COMPANY 8th SERVICE BATTALION
EAST SURREY REGIMENT
AND DRIBBLED INTO THE GERMAN
TRENCHES AT THE ASSAULT
AND CAPTURE OF MONTAUBAN
JULY 1st 1916.
(COPYRIGHT.)

9 Prisoners of War

LARGE NUMBERS OF prisoners of war (POWs) were captured between 1914 and 1918. By far the most were from Russia (3,910,000), while Austria-Hungary fared little better (2,118,190). The Germans, who were fighting on both the Western and Eastern Fronts, had 993,180 men captured. The Allies, who were fighting mainly on the Western Front, had fewer of their men as POWs. Those countries with over 2,000 men in captivity included France (446,300), the United Kingdom (170,389), India (11,070), Belgium (10,200) and Canada (2,820).

PLATE 83 PRIVATE THOMAS CORNELL 514355 (LEFT) – A BRITISH POW

Thomas Cornell was born in Huddersfield and later worked as a grocer in Garrett Lane, Tooting, London. When he enlisted on 8 September 1915 he was married to Louise and they had one child. Thomas was captured on 25 September 1917 in a trench raid by the Germans on the British positions near Laynicourt-Marcel. He was sent to Henberg POW camp, which was used in both world wars. Thomas was repatriated back to Britain on 7 January 1919.

PLATE 84

The card, passed by the field censor, was postally used on 14 January 1916 and sent to Irene, c/o Mrs Wright, 21 Portobello Road, Notting Hill, London.

> 'Dear Rene
> Here's some German prisoners for you. Look after Mam for me. Heaps of Love from Dad.'

PLATE 84 **THE WORLD WAR 1914–15**
German prisoners captured after the fighting in Ville-sur-Tourbe (west of Verdun) march through Chalons-sur-Marne (north-east of Laval).

PLATE 85 **GUERRE 1914–15**
The French card, not postally used, shows German prisoners captured in the woods surrounding Cœuvres, near Soissons.

PLATE 86 NOEUX-LES-MINES

The card, not postally used but dated 17 June 1916 on the back, shows two German officers in Noeux-les-Mines, just south of Bethune, who were captured after the fighting.

PLATE 87 THE RESULT OF HARD BATTLE – GERMAN PRISONERS OF WAR AT VERDUN

PLATE 88

On the back of the card it states:

> 'Official photograph taken by the photographic section of the French army issued by NEWSPAPER ILLUSTRATIONS Ltd, 161a Strand, (London), WC.
>
> The result of hard battle – German prisoners of war at Verdun – The German soldiers are gradually being captured in ever increasing numbers, and many appear to be mighty pleased when they are labelled "Prisoners of War".'

The card, which was not postally used, was sold in aid of the YMCA Hut Fund.

PLATE 89 GERMAN PRISONERS AND THEIR GUARDS

The card was posted from Dorchester, Dorset on 7 October to a London address. Jack writes:

> 'Expect me tomorrow Friday Jack.'

Could it be that Jack was one of the guards and the prisoners were marching through Dorchester?

PLATE 90 BACK OF THOMAS CORNELL CARD (SEE PLATE 83)

Thomas Cornell sent this card to his wife from the POW camp to give her his address. His camp number – 20208 – is visible on his tunic.

PLATE 91 GERMAN POW CARD

This humorous German card, published by Dr Eyster & Co., 'publisher of funny papers, GMBH Berlin S.W. 68' and sent on 28 May 1915 depicts the Allies as a ragbag bunch that included French, English, Scots, Indians, Africans and Canadians, among others (there is even a Red Indian in the group).

PLATE 92 LES VILLAS DE LA PLAGE ET LES PLANCHES, WIMEREUX – L.L.

10 Cards from Somewhere in France – 1917

PLATE 92

Wimereux is on the coast, just north of Boulogne-Sur-Mer and thus well back from the front. ERTD writes:

> 'I'm back at the old Depot again where I remain until my kit turns up, at present it's on its way out to France. I visited G's hospital the other evening and took Margaret Deane out to dinner. I'm glad you like the Imperial. I wonder when I shall be in Blighty again, a fortnight perhaps! any how I'm going to get back to the Battle of the Swamps. ERTD.'

The French card is dated 3 November 1917 and an indentation in the card shows that it was posted in an envelope.

PLATE 93 THE *BRIGHTON QUEEN* LEAVING THE PORT AT BOULOGNE-SUR-MER – L.L.

PLATE 93

The *Brighton Queen* also sailed from Eastbourne, Sussex. She was built in 1897 by the Clydebank Shipping and Engineering Company for the Brighton, Worthing and South Coast Steamboat Company. She stood 240 foot in length, with 553 gross tonnage and a maximum speed of 20 knots. The ship made numerous cross-Channel excursions but sadly had a relatively short life. She was requisitioned by the Admiralty in September 1914, and on the night of 5 October 1915, during mine-sweeping duties off the Belgian coast, she struck a mine and sank.

The card was sent on 22 January 1917 to Swansea, South Wales from BEF Somewhere! As such, it would seem that the card was still for sale 16 months after the vessel's demise.

> 'Hope you'll get my letter posted yesterday. We've had no more snow but plenty of frost – has not thawed yet, I might get your parcel up tonight generally takes 5–6 days or so: will let you know. Hope my little girly is still keeping well, also your dear D & M. still getting sufficient "graft" to keep me going along wonderful where the work all comes from. All my love, Kisses xxxx'

PLATE 94 A STATION IN THE NORTH OF FRANCE – THE INDIAN ARMY LOAD MULES ON TO THE TRAIN

PLATE 95 WAR 1914–16 – RUINS AFTER THE BOMBARDMENT

PLATE 94

The French card is not dated and was sent home in an envelope.

> 'Dearest Maud just a few lines hoping you are quite well as it leaves me at present I rec fags safe today I was quiet pleased to get them We are having snow again so it is quite cold again. Dear Maud thiss is the kind of correags we were in for a night and a day when we got here first and that is how we had to put our horses in.'

In 'Sketches of Tommy's Life', Fergus Mackain depicts soldiers travelling in horse trucks, with forty men or eight horses per truck ('Hommes 40 Chevaux 8').

PLATE 95

The card posted on 25 March 1917 to Mrs Matt Sheppard, 75 Vickers Road, Sheffield shows mules sheltering among the ruins of buildings destroyed by a bombardment in the Somme region.

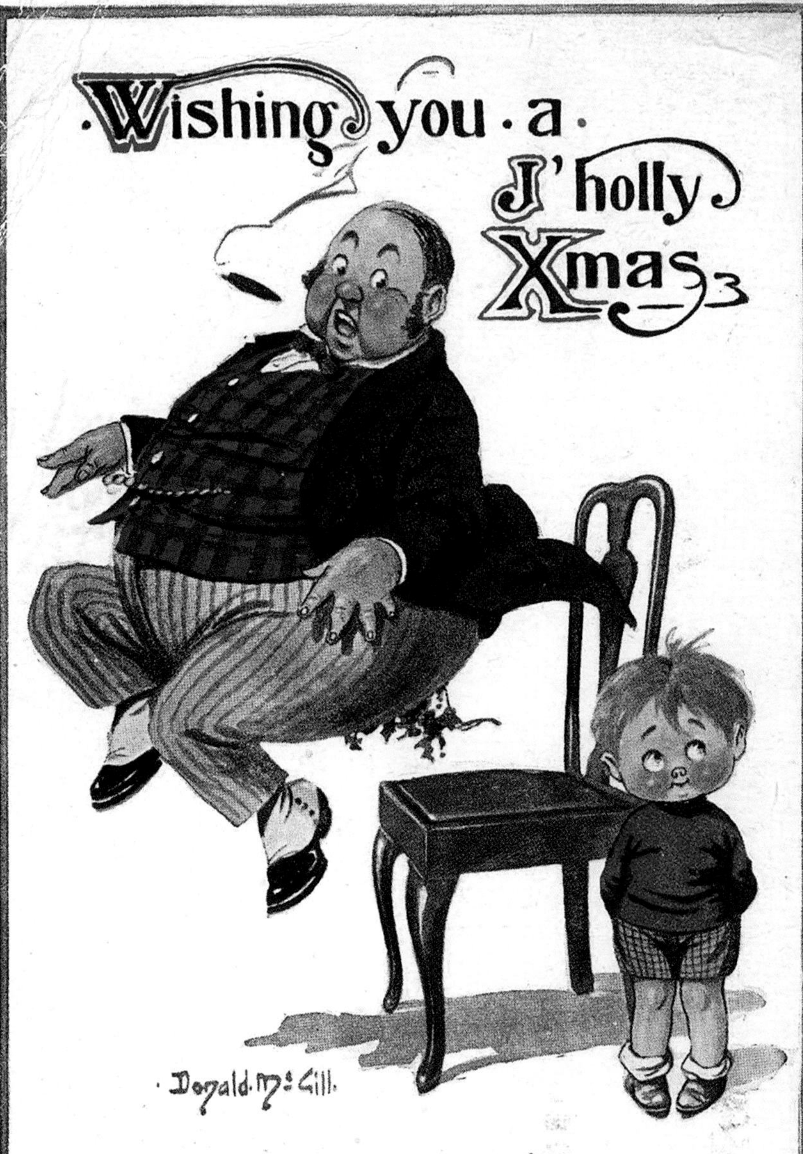
Wishing you a
J'holly
Xmas
Donald McGill
— and hoping you'll
"rise to the occasion" well.

11 Christmas

In December 1914, King George V and Queen Mary sent a Christmas card to accompany the magnificent gift from Princess Mary of a brass box containing cigarettes and tobacco or, for non-smokers, a writing case and sweets or drops and for the nurses at the front, chocolates. Also enclosed was one of two royal postcards, depicting George in either an army or naval uniform (depending on the service of the recipient) and a version for convalescing soldiers with the message 'May you soon be restored to health'. The standard box contained a pipe, tobacco, a lighter, twenty monogrammed cigarettes, and a picture of Princess Mary. Alternative versions were produced for minority groups to consider dietary rules of religions and as supplies ran short, many gift boxes ended up with a number of variations.

PLATE 96 'WISHING YOU A J'HOLLY XMAS'

This Donald McGill card was passed by the censor and posted on 19 December 1917 to Master Wallie Wale, 11 Lake Street, Oxford, England.

> 'Dear Wallie, Many thanks for your nice letter & drawing you are getting quite clever, although I think you are inclined to be like the boy on this card. Love from Uncle Harry.'

PLATE 97 THE ROYAL SUSSEX REGIMENT

A card printed in England by Gale & Polden Ltd, London, Aldershot and Portsmouth was used to send Christmas wishes from Dowager Lady Loder to the officers of the 4th Battalion. Lady Loder owned Leonardslee House, Horsham during the war. The date the card was sent is unknown as the regiment served in Gallipoli and Palestine until 1918, when they were brought over to the Western Front during the German spring offensive in 1918.

THE ROYAL SUSSEX REGIMENT.

(35th Foot and 107th Foot.)

BATTLE HONOURS.

The United Red and White Rose.
The White (Rousillon) Plume.

"Gibraltar, 1704-05." "Louisburg." "Quebec, 1759." "Martinique, 1762." "Havannah." "St. Lucia, 1778." "Maida." "Egypt, 1882." "Nile, 1884-85." "Abu Klea." "South Africa, 1900-02."

THE ROYAL SUSSEX REGT.

HISTORY AND TRADITIONS.

The Regiment was raised by the Earl of Donegal in 1701, and first saw service at the siege of Gibraltar in 1704, and as soon as the siege was raised took part in the capture and defence of Barcelona in 1706. It was nearly destroyed at the battle of Almanza in 1707. In 1759 it was with Wolfe at the capture of Quebec, where its gallantry won the white plume now commemorated in the Regimental Badge. It served in the campaign in Holland in 1799, in the capture of Malta in 1800, and at the battle of Maida in 1806. It did excellent service during the Indian Mutiny, suffering severely from all the hardships it went through. In 1882 it took part in the Egyptian campaign, and in 1884 in the Nile Expedition. It was fighting in India again in 1888, also in 1897-8. It was engaged in the South African War, including the hard won fights at Diamond Hill and Wittebergen.

NICKNAME.

"The Orange Lilles," from its facings and plume.

PLATE 97 THE ROYAL SUSSEX REGIMENT

PLATE 98 BACK OF CARD

Printed in England by GALE & POLDEN, LTD., London, Aldershot, and Portsmouth (Copyright.)

POST CARD. (For Address only.)

BRITISH PRINTING.

Leonardslee
Horsham

Lady Loder sends you best Christmas wishes & hopes you keep well. She is sure you are proud of your Regiment We all look forward to the time when God sends "Peace on Earth" to see you safe back in England —

70

PLATE 99 'ALL CHRISTMAS JOY BE THINE'

This Valentines series card was not postally used but may well have been purchased in 1914. The *Daily News* ran an appeal to raise funds to provide soldiers at the front with Christmas puddings. On a card, sent on 20 December 1916, the Editor sent his thanks to the Fulham Baptist 'Men's Own & Friends' for a donation of £1 2s. 6d., which would provide fifty-three puddings.

Private Cecil Withers (1898–2005) quoted in *The Last Post*, said, 'The *Daily Mail* used to send two-pound tins of Christmas pudding for us at the front. They sent them every Christmas, and the officers would wait on the men for their Christmas dinner.'

Like Albert Marshall (plate 66), Cecil Withers was wounded at the front, evacuated to hospital in England and then sent to a convalescent camp in Cornwall. He then returned to the trenches in France.

PLATE 100 XMAS GREETINGS

The card, slightly larger than the standard size, is a copy of a painting by war artist James Prinsep Barnes Beadle, the son of Major General James Pattle Beadle. Entitled 'Going to the trenches', it features the 7th Division, who had fought at Ypres, Neuve Chapelle, Festubert and Loos. On the back, a father wrote 'Merry Xmas to Norman'.

PLATE 101 THANKS FROM SIR D. HAIG, SEPTEMBER 1916

PLATE 102 'WELL! HERE'S LUCK TO YOU ALL THIS XMAS & MAY THE ENTENTE BE CONTENT'

The card was sent on 22 December 1916 from East Dulwich, London to miss Eva Monday, 121 Green Lanes, Stoke Newington, London.

> 'Dear Eva, Just to wish you a very happy Xmas Love from K Sargent.'

The Christmas pudding is adorned with the flags of (from left to right) Russia, France, Great Britain, Belgium, Japan and Serbia.

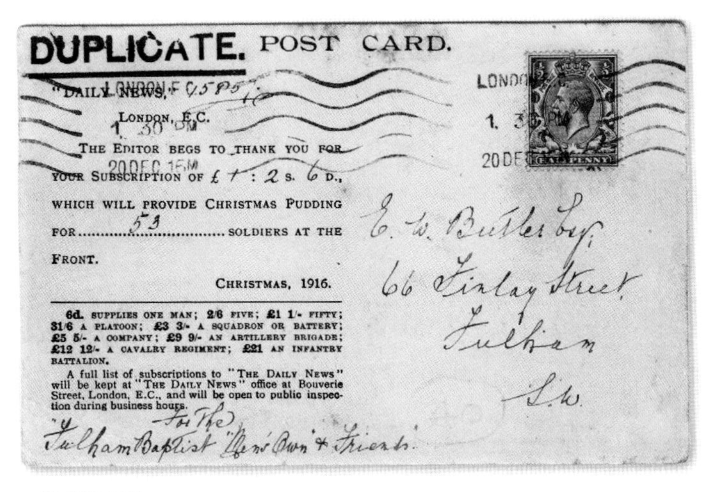

DUPLICATE. POST CARD.

"DAILY NEWS,"
LONDON, E.C.

THE EDITOR BEGS TO THANK YOU FOR YOUR SUBSCRIPTION OF £ 1 : 2 S. 6 D., WHICH WILL PROVIDE CHRISTMAS PUDDING FOR ......53...... SOLDIERS AT THE FRONT.

CHRISTMAS, 1916.

6d. SUPPLIES ONE MAN; 2/6 FIVE; £1 1/- FIFTY; 31/6 A PLATOON; £3 3/- A SQUADRON OR BATTERY; £5 5/- A COMPANY; £9 9/- AN ARTILLERY BRIGADE; £12 12/- A CAVALRY REGIMENT; £21 AN INFANTRY BATTALION.

A full list of subscriptions to "THE DAILY NEWS" will be kept at "THE DAILY NEWS" office at Bouverie Street, London, E.C., and will be open to public inspection during business hours.

PLATE 103

PLATE 104

Some Christmas good wishes did not arrive. This card of Nuns Walk in Winchester, sent from Hove, Sussex on 11 December 1917 by Evelyn Pearson to Fraulein Heiss, Waldheim, Berne, Switzerland was rejected and returned by the censor. We can only guess why this was so, as Switzerland was a neutral country during both world wars.

> 'This is to wish you both as happy a Xmas as possible and a happier and more peaceful New Year. Love to you and Fraulein Mina from Evelyn Pearson.'

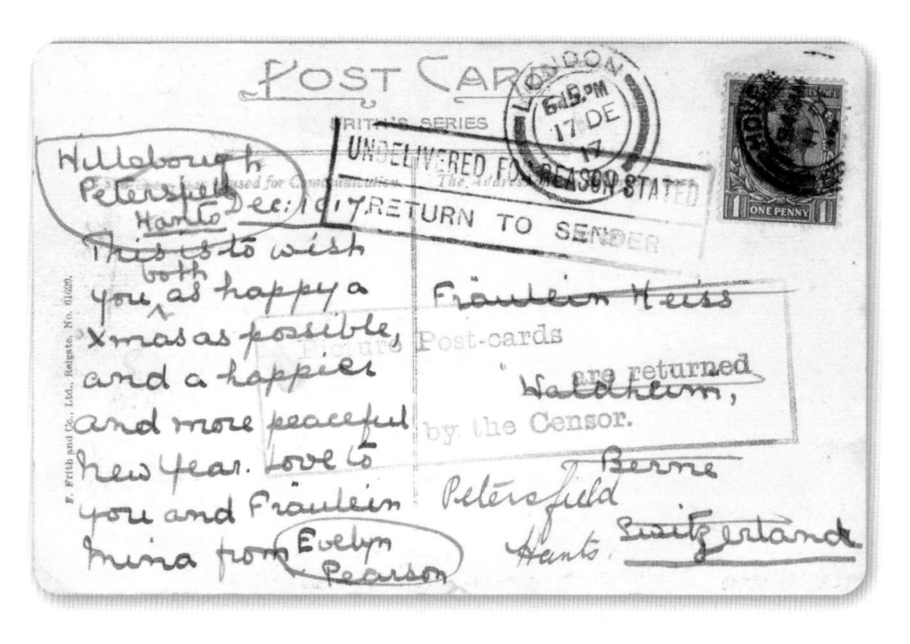
POST CARD
FRITH'S SERIES
LONDON 6.15 PM 17 DE 17
UNDELIVERED FOR REASON STATED
RETURN TO SENDER
ONE PENNY
F. Frith and Co., Ltd., Reigate. No. 61620.

Hillsborough
Petersfield
Hants
This is to wish you both as happy a Xmas as possible, and a happier and more peaceful New Year. Love to you and Fräulein Mina from Evelyn Pearson

~~Fräulein Heiss~~
~~Waldheim,~~
~~Berne~~
~~Switzerland~~
Petersfield
Hants.

Picture Post-cards are returned by the Censor.

PLATE 105 FINISH JOHNNY! – GREETINGS FROM SALONIKA ARMY, CHRISTMAS 1918

At the Salonika Front, a multinational force held the Bulgarians at Sulva Bay in mountainous northern Greece. They were often considered a forgotten army. The maintenance of the Salonika Front cost almost 500,000 casualties – 18,000 from the war, the rest from disease.[15]

FINISH JOHNNY!

GREETINGS FROM THE

SALONIKA ARMY

XMAS - 1918.

8th Field Survey Coy. R.E. No. 529.

PLATE 106 LE BAC DE TROUVILLE-DEAUVILLE

PLATE 107 RUE DU PHARE, CAYEUX-SUR-MER

The card was posted on 29 September 1918 and sent to Mr H. Thornicroft, 44 Pinnes Road, Harrow.

> 'Dear Harry, I suppose you have gone back to school now. Do write soon I will send you another PC soon.'

12 Cards from Somewhere in France - January-November 1918

Soldiers often worried about the health and welfare of their wives and sweethearts. There was the threat from air raids, especially in London and the South East, the dreaded influenza epidemic, and a lack of food and coal for heating and cooking. There was even the probability that their loved one had found somebody else.

On 7 January 1918, Billy wrote to his wife in Wolverhampton:

'My dearest

Still not a line from you and I am getting most anxious as to whether there is anything the matter. The next letter you send would you Register it my dear & see if this will give you any result. I'm still going along well & keeping fit. What kind of weather are you having my chick. It is still very severe with us, but they tell us the end of the month should see the worst of it over. Do let me have a line as quickly as you can. All my love and kisses Billy.'

PLATE 106

The card was passed by the censor, who did not erase the name of the towns as they were in a safe area well back from the front. On 11 March 1918, A.J. Green wrote:

'Convalescent here after being "gassed" by Fritz. Hope this will find you as I believe you have altered the name of the cop. Kindest regards I am Yrs. Sincerely A J Green.'

The card was sent to J. Sutherland, The Provident Clerks, 27–29 Moorgate Street, London.

KORTRIJK
De Post
IN DER BEURS

13 Cards From Somewhere – Armistice to Peace Treaty (11 November 1918 – 28 June 1919)

CARDS WERE NOT only posted in France. Under the terms of the Armistice, the Allies had to enter the previously occupied territories of Belgium and France and then Germany itself as far as the River Rhine. If the peace talks had broken down, the war could have flared up again and the Allies could not afford to stand down their armies until peace was secured.

PLATE 108 KORTRIJK, BELGIUM
27 November 1918 (16 days after the Armistice)

The card was sent to Mrs Oldfield, 15 Lewisham High Road, New Cross, London, and had been passed by the censor, who was no longer required to erase the name of the town.

'Dear Mrs Oldfield
Your welcome letter to hand. Glad to hear you are all well. We have been staying at a village about 2 miles from this town (Courtrai) for nearly a fortnight. We are now allowed to state where we are, so I thought you would like a few PCs. Shall write in a few days. Best wishes Alex.'

PLATE 109 GRAMMONT, FRANCE (NEAR TO THE GERMAN BORDER) – 8 DECEMBER 1918

PLATE 110 CHARLEROI, BELGIUM – 12 DECEMBER 1918

PLATE 109

Card sent to Miss Williams, 94 Copleston Road, East Dulwich, London:

> 'Dear Miss W
> Now that the fighting is over things seem very quiet. I am seeing many new towns and villages and hope soon to be in Germany. Hope you are well yours sincerely (signature?)'

A very formal card, with no love or kisses (as yet!).

PLATE 110

The card was sent to Mrs C.W. Mynn, 76 Victoria Road, Alexandra Park, London:

> 'Dear T.
> We reached here today. We are billeted in a school one minute from the bandstand as shown in the view. We move on again tomorrow. Will write when we get settled C.'

PLATE 111 LE COUVENT, LIÈGE, BELGIUM – 13 DECEMBER 1918

Card sent to Miss E. Cashmore, Kenyon House, Leopold Street, Loughborough, Leics.

> '9/10.12.18
> My billet on the date above. Received a warm welcome from the sisters of the True Cross, three of whom were English. Passed a happy half hour listening to the children sing. B.L.E.'

PLATE 112
BLANKENHEIM (EIFEL), GERMANY – 17 DECEMBER 1918

'Fred' sent the card to Miss M. Beddon, Belmere House, Welshampton, Ellesmere, Salop.

> 'My Dear Mary,
> Thanks so much for your dear letter. Yes I received the camera safely also the other good things for which many thanks. Do please forgive my not writing a letter as we are continually on the move. We have been marching for 11 days continuously except for one days halt 4 days ago. One doesn't feel much like writing Love Fred.'

PLATE 113

Tommy sent the card to his mother, Mrs Anne Jones, Fair View, Newbury, Anglesey, North Wales.

> 'Dear Ma Received your letter safe. Will write a letter tomorrow. The shop marked X is where I bought PC Well Ta Ta now I remain your dear son Tommy.'

PLATE 114

Sent to J.A. Shaftoe Esq., Coney Street, York from Corporal Shaftoe 54253 L. Sigs Bn. R.E., GHQ.

> '16.1.9 Arrived here this morning and wound up my watch over the Rhine on one of these bridges which are marvels. I return tonight late. Best wishes Law.'

PLATE 113 THE VILLAGE OF BURSCHEID, GERMANY – 10 JANUARY 1919

PLATE 114 COLOGNE, GERMANY (ON THE RIVER RHINE) – 17 JANUARY 1919

WE 'LL
"DELIVER
THE GOODS"
MORE
MUNITIO
WANTE
Donald McGill.
"— YES, AN' IT AINT A BIT LIKE KNITTIN' SOCKS EITHER !! "

14 Women Munitions Workers

WOMEN PLAYED A, vital role in Royal Ordnance Factories and national shell-filling factories, as well as in other engineering, metal-working and aircraft industries. It was dangerous work and not a bit like knitting socks!

PLATE 115 'YES, AN IT AINT A BIT LIKE KNITTIN' SOCKS EITHER!!'

On a card sent from Nottingham on 23 August 1915 to Mrs Ross Junior, 53 Hales Bar, Haleswood, near Sheffield, Mum wrote:

> 'My dear Lizzy I expect I shall be meeting you doing something like this, they are starting a large munition place in Nottingham so look out – '

The 'munition place' may well have been the National Shell Filling Factory at Chilwell, a few miles south-west of Nottingham. Women made up a large part of the workforce at the Chilwell factory.[16]

To the Cherished Memory of

ENGLAND'S

Gallant Munition Girls

Who bravely did their duty, working and singing from morning till night, making shells for Tommy and Jack, and helping to win the war. They laid down their lives for King and Country, JULY 1st, 1918, and they could do no more. Sadly missed by all who knew and loved them.—" Peace, Perfect Peace."

A sudden change—they in a moment fell,
They had not time to bid their friends farewell,
Death quickly came—without a warning given,
And bid them haste to meet their God in Heaven.

Composed by G. McDONNELL.

PLATE 116 ENGLAND'S GALLANT MUNITION GIRLS (SEE PAGE 98)

Munitions girls were nicknamed 'Canaries' as handling TNT could stain one's skin yellow. On 1 July 1918 a catastrophic explosion tore through the Chilwell factory. The blast killed 134 workers and injured 250 more – the biggest loss of life from a single accidental explosion during the First World War. Of the 134 dead, twenty-five were women. The card celebrates the lives of these gallant munition girls.

PLATE 117 MUNITIONS WORKERS

PLATE 118 THREE MUNITIONS WORKERS

PLATE 119 THEY WANT TO TAKE MY BADGE AWAY

All the female workers in the two photographs above are wearing triangular 'ON WAR SERVICE' badges. These were issued to those in vital work on the home front so that they were not perceived as shirkers and, in the case of men, not pestered by the White Feather Campaign. The two men in the group photograph have round 'ON WAR SERVICE' badges, as shown on the card from a drawing by the war artist Fred Spurgin. The card was not postally used until 14 August 1928. E.J. writes, 'Having a ripping time at Cleethorpes. E.J.'

8 CARDS

Daily Mail

OFFICIAL WAR POSTCARDS

[Crown Copyright Reserved.]

8 CARDS

The Press Bureau has granted to *The Daily Mail* the exclusive right to reproduce the wonderful official photographs of the British Army fighting on the Western Front.

The Daily Mail will hand over to the Press Bureau half the nett profits from the publication of these postcards, and has guaranteed a minimum payment of £5,000. The money is to be devoted to military charities.

SERIES

Containing the following 8 cards in silver print style:—
(PHOTOGRAPHIC FACSIMILE)

No. 73 Happy "Tommies" wearing Hun Helmets
" 74 Church Service before Battle.
" 75 A British heavy gun in action.
" 76 The Worcesters going into action.
" 77 "Tommy" finds shell holes comfortable to sleep in.
" 78 After the first cavalry charge, July, 1916.
" 79 Firing a heavy howitzer in France.
" 80 Australians parading for the trenches.

6D. PER PACKET

Published by the Associated Newspapers, Ltd., Carmelite [illegible] London, E.C.

6D. PER PACKET.

PLATE 120 ***DAILY MAIL*** **OFFICIAL WAR POSTCARDS**

PLATE 121 THE KING AT THE FRONT – 'THE SMILE OF VICTORY' (SERIES XI, NO. 81)
'The Smile of Victory' is composed of an historic group. From left to right: General Joffre, President Poincare of France, King George V, General Foch and Sir Douglas Haig.

15 Newspaper Campaigns

MANY BRITISH NEWSPAPERS, organised campaigns to raise funds in order to provide 'comforts' for the troops. One of the most noteworthy was that of the Daily Mail. The newspaper issued a total of 176 photographic postcards in sets of eight. Each of the sets were sold for 6d. (2.5p).

The cards were issued in three formats: colour, sepia and black and white. Some cards were produced at different times, in more than one format and with different numbers.

Demand for these war postcards was intense and many, if not most, found their way into special albums issued by the newspaper in October 1916, selling for 2s. and 6d. (12.5p). The albums were designed to hold 240 cards. It is not surprising to note that most of the Daily Mail cards found today were not postally used and were not sent back from the front.

PLATE 122 THE KING AT THE FRONT – A GREETING FROM THE TROOPS (SERIES XII, NO. 96)

PLATE 123 DECORATING A CANADIAN ON THE FIELD OF BATTLE (SERIES VII, NO. 50)

Decoration on the field is an honour coveted by soldiers. The picture shows a brave Canadian Lance Corporal receiving the Distinguished Conduct Medal. The card was sent on 7 November 1916 from Stoke Newington to Miss C.E. Salmon, Lynsted, Hillcrest Road, Purley, Surrey.

'Many happy returns of the Day. W.H.S.'

PLATE 124 HAPPY 'TOMMIES' WEARING HUN HELMETS (SERIES X, NO. 73)

'The possession of a German helmet delights "Tommy" and such trophies have become very common in the Big Push. Several are worn by the smiling troops.'

Could the soldier on the right of the front row be another 'trophy'? He would seem to be being held in position.

PLATE 125 HELPING AN AMBULANCE THROUGH THE MUD (SERIES I, NO. 5)
'Heavy rains have often made the British Front a quagmire, and our "Tommies" have had to put their shoulders to the wheels of ambulance and other wagons.'

PLATE 126 A PRESENT FOR THE KAISER (SERIES XVI, NO. 122)
'Our grand artillerymen like to address a shell before they fire it. This shell, being of the biggest size, is addressed to the Biggest Hun.'

PLATE 127 'ARF A MO KAISER!'

During the war, cigarettes were brought up with the rations as most of the troops smoked. In fact, smoking was positively encouraged, with most Princess Mary boxes containing cigarettes and tobacco. The *Weekly Dispatch* newspaper organised a campaign to raise money for a 'tobacco fund', with the help of a postcard specially drawn by war artist Bert Thomas, who had drawn cartoons for *Punch* and the *Evening News*.

The back of the card states:

> 'Specially drawn by Mr BERT THOMAS for the "WEEKLY DISPATCH" TOBACCO FUND, Carmelite Housel London, E C. Every 6d will gladden the heart of a hero.'

The card first appeared in December 1914, and over the next four years it helped to raise £250,000 (equivalent to 10 million sixpences).

PLATE 128 CANADA FINDS A LITTLE DOG IN HUN TRENCHES & PRESENTS IT TO NURSE

The *Daily Mirror* negotiated a deal with the Canadian authorities to issue its own brand of photographic postcards based on Canadian official war photographs.[17]

On the back it states:

> 'THE *DAILY MIRROR* CANADIAN OFFICIAL SERIES (photograph passed by censor). Photogravure series. Printed in Great Britain. Published by the Pictorial Newspaper Co. (1910) Ltd, 23/9 Bouverie Street, London, England.'

The card was posted from Bridlington Station on 7 July 1917 to Mr F. Pocklington, c/o Barclays Bank, Silver Street, Hull.

> 'Dear Frank, we arrived here last Sat. So one week has almost gone. If weather keeps nice think we shall stay the month. I understand Hull is not far away, could you not cycle over on Sunday? Let me know beforehand if you do. It is such a nice time. Write as soon as poss. Fondest love from Edith.'

PLATE 129 BUYING WAR BONDS AT THE TANK IN TRAFALGAR SQUARE, LONDON
Here, tank Nelson (no. 130) is pictured near Nelson's column, with one of the famous lions just visible on the left side of the photograph. The card in the Valentine's series was not postally used.[27]

PLATE 130 OUR TANK BANK

16 Financing the War

PLATE 130

Following the debut of two Mark IV tanks at the Lord Mayor's Show in London during November 1917, the British government mobilised examples of these 'wonder machines' to raise money and support for the sale of war bonds and War Savings Certificates. Nelson (no. 130) was one of six Mark IV male tanks that were on tour in Britain in 1918, raising millions of pounds through 'Tank Bank Weeks'. Each tank became the focal point for donations. After a stint in London, Nelson was located in Huddersfield between 18 and 23 February 1918.

On the back of another card, featuring tank Nelson, Nora wrote:

> 'Dear Tilly
> Many thanks for your pretty p.c. we are having much better weather here just now.
>
> I was sorry to hear about your boys being taken prisoners of war it does seem a pity. I knew such a lot of our boys who have fallen in the battlefield also there are quite a number who have been lost at sea. One bonnie little boy only sixteen having been left several days in an open boat without water or food and he expired when rescued. I thought this was one of the worst cases I had read. You see, he lived very near us.
>
> I am sending you this PC of the tank as we had Nelson here a fortnight ago & we raised a – amount of war loans £12 – 10s in all per head. With love Nora.'

The card would have been sent in 1918. Unfortunately, we are not able to tell where Nora lived or where tank Nelson visited.

PLATE 131 FEED THE GUNS

The placard states 'Feed the guns with War Bonds and help to end the War.' On the back of the card, not dated and posted in an envelope, a father wrote:

'Dear Ruth, just a PC of the Square during Feed the Guns week not so good as I should like to have sent you but it is something to remind you of the Great War Dad with love xxx'

PLATE 132 'BUY NATIONAL WAR BONDS' / 'BUY NATIONAL WAR BONDS NOW'

Two cards franked in May 1918 exhorted the public to 'Buy National War Bonds' and 'Buy National War Bonds Now'.

Posted on 27 May 1918 the Donald McGill card (no. 2193) was not war related and was sent to Master Robin Lockerby, 39 Howarth Street, Old Trafford, Manchester from Marfa Cottage, 10 Church Street, Rhyl.

'Dear Robin,
I am having a nice holiday at Rhyll because I have been very ill. Nora is going to School to get her certificate but will get her holiday later. Love to all Aunt Marie.'

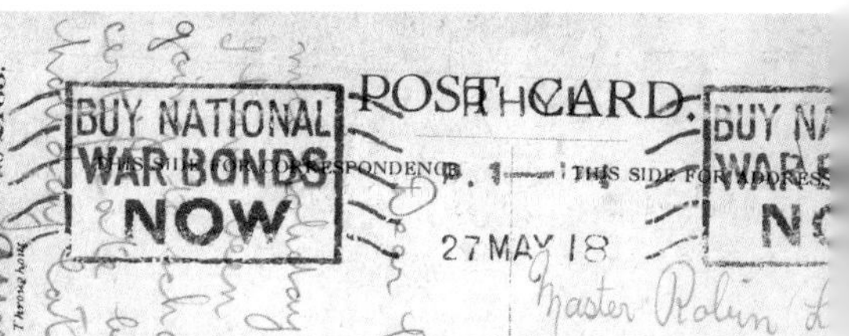

PLATE 133 BRITISH FLYING BOATS

With the formation of the Ministry of Information in 1918 came an official series of propaganda cards promoting the sale of war bonds. The cards, priced 1d., were issued by A.M. Davis and Co. of Finsbury Square, London.

'From materials supplied by the Ministry of Information. Passed by censor. Printed in England.'

Design no. 11 showed two British flying boats. The card states that our National Savings investment of 15s. 6d. (77.5p) could be redeemed at a later date for £1.

PLATE 134 WAR BOND CAMPAIGN POSTCARD

OUT FOR VICTORY.
THE FARM GIRL.
Who is doing her bit to feed us all.

PLATE 135 OUT FOR VICTORY – THE FARM GIRL

Another form of service was given by those who provided gifts to the troops serving at the front or provided funds for the building and running of huts provided by the Church Army, the YMCA and other charitable organisations.

As well as financing the war, those on the home front were encouraged to give service in factories, on farms and, for those too old to fight, by producing food from their allotments. With the slogan 'Dig for victory', it aimed to counter the loss of food imports caused by German U boat action.

PLATE 136 CHURCH ARMY RECREATION HUT

On a card posted on 9 January 1916 to Miss Welch, 328 New Road, High Walton, near Preston and passed by the censor, a soldier wrote:

> 'Dear Friend, Just a few lines hoping you are keeping well. You will know I have joined our Battallion ready to go up to the trenches when they go in again. It is very muddy out here but all the men are cheerfull. I hope you got all the parcels off allright and that they all got them. I hope we shall meet again some day. You can send me a pair of socks now and then when they send me a parcel. I remain your friend J Swift.'

PLATE 137 INTERIOR OF YMCA CENTRAL HUT, FOVANT (ON THE A30, SOUTH-WEST OF WILTON, WILTSHIRE)

Hot and cold drinks were available, as were Bible classes. The card was sent by Fred to his mother.

PLATE 138 BRITISH AND BELGIAN SOLDIERS PREPARE A MEAL

PLATE 139 YMCA HUT FUND

PLATE 138

Cards sold in aid of the YMCA Hut Fund or issued by the YMCA Hut Fund 'to provide Comforts, Shelter and Recreation for our soldiers. Collect the full series of 312 cards, they form an historical collection.'

Most of the cards in the series were collected and few are found postally used. Unfortunately, the cards were not numbered.

Donald McGill
She accepted my Flowers, my Sweets, my Cash and — my Rival !!
Elle a accepté mes fleurs, mes bonbons, mon argent,—et mon rival!

17 'Your Country Needs You'

FROM THE START of hostilities, Donald McGill and other postcard artists did their best to help the drive for volunteers to enlist. After the early flood of volunteers, conscription for single men was introduced in January 1916, and in April it was extended to married men between the ages of 18 and 41 years. Those who did not enlist of their own volition began to be targeted by all kinds of insidious propaganda. McGill used the trick of putting children in situations which could then be transferred to adults, and in particular he used the theme of girls only choosing to give their affections to soldiers and sailors in uniform.

PLATE 140 'SHE ACCEPTED MY FLOWERS, MY SWEETS, MY CASH AND ... MY RIVAL!' (ALSO IN FRENCH)

The card was written on Monday 11 October 1918.

> 'Dear Wife, Got your letter last night good war news will not be long in beeing home. In good spirits everybody pleased. I am champion From your loving husband Frank.'

The same theme was deployed in the card 'No Gun – No Girl' (plate 141).

PLATE 141 'NO GUN – NO GIRL!' (ALSO IN FRENCH)

The card is dated 21 October 1916. Children, even girls, are shown as being desperate to enlist and do their bit, the implication being that young men should be ready to do this as a matter of course.

PLATE 142 'DEAR LORD, IF YOU'RE STILL MAKING LITTLE BOYS CAN'T I BE CHANGED INTO ONE – NOW?' (ALSO IN FRENCH)

The McGill card was posted on 27 April 1917 from the Western Front to Goldington, Bedfordshire.

The overwhelming strength of public opinion was behind the war and so those who were most reviled for not enlisting were the conscientious objectors.

PLATE 143 THE COLD SHOULDER

The card was not postally used.

PLATE 144 'OH WELL, I'M DOING MY BIT.'

We don't think much of the man who has not enlisted and who has only donated one penny to help pay for the war. On the back, Connie wrote:

> 'Many happy returns on your Birthday. With love from Connie xxx'

PLATE 145 'THANK THE LORD I AINT GOT A CONSCIENCE!' (ALSO IN FRENCH)

The Donald McGill card in the Artistique series (no. 1431) is interesting for a number of reasons. The name of the recipient has been erased. The card was sent on 15 November 1919, after the peace treaty of 28 June 1919, from Belgium to an address in The Hague, The Netherlands. Could it be that the recipient had fled Belgium for the safety of a neutral country?

It would greatly assist the collectors of eggs for the wounded soldiers if, upon coming to Church, each lady would lay an egg in the Font!

18 Wartime Artists

THREE MEN DESERVE special mention. Donald McGill is perhaps the most famous of all postcard artists, mostly because of his prolific output. He worked as a naval draughtsman until his career in postcards began accidentally in 1904, after drawing a get-well card for a sick nephew. Within a year this was to become his full-time occupation, which lasted until his death in 1962. It is estimated that McGill produced over 12,000 designs.

McGill's wartime output is well-observed and well-drawn, despite having no first-hand knowledge of life at the front. This was partly due to him being 40 years old in January 1915. More to the point, McGill was mad about sport and had sustained an injury to his left ankle during a rugby match when he was 16. By the time he was persuaded to see a doctor the damaged bone in his foot was so diseased that he had to have the foot amputated. McGill would never have been passed fit for service at the front.

Books on Donald McGill include: *Wish You Were Here: The Art of Donald McGill* (1966), *The World of Donald McGill* (1984), *Donald McGill Postcard Artist* (2014) and *McGill's War* (2014).

Once recruits had joined the armed forces, basic training began. This is well portrayed by Donald McGill through a large number of postcards available throughout the war years.

PLATE 146 IT WOULD GREATLY ASSIST THE COLLECTORS OF EGGS

PLATE 146

This card in the 'Comique' series (no. 1993) was a reprint; rather than asking for eggs for the poor, this time they were requested for wounded soldiers.

Ted, on active service, was most likely in the Royal Navy. He wrote to his mother, Mrs Wilson, Desford Lane, Kirkby Mallory, Nr Hickley, Leicestershire.

'Dear Mother,
Just a P.C. asking you please send time table, I am thinking of coming up if possible if they give the week end to my watch in a fortnights time, it would only mean Saturday night to Sunday at home but it would kill time bit. Best of love Ted.'

PLATE 147 'AND THEN WE HAVE ALL THE REST OF THE DAY TO OURSELVES'

The card was sent from Marlborough Lines on 23 February 1915 to Miss P. Kneeshaw, North Gate, Market Weighton, East Yorkshire.

> 'Dear P, I thought I would just write to let you know that we have started off today. So I will let you know when we arrive. Happy as a King. Hoping you are the same from yours …'

It may have been that the writer was off to France in the next draft.

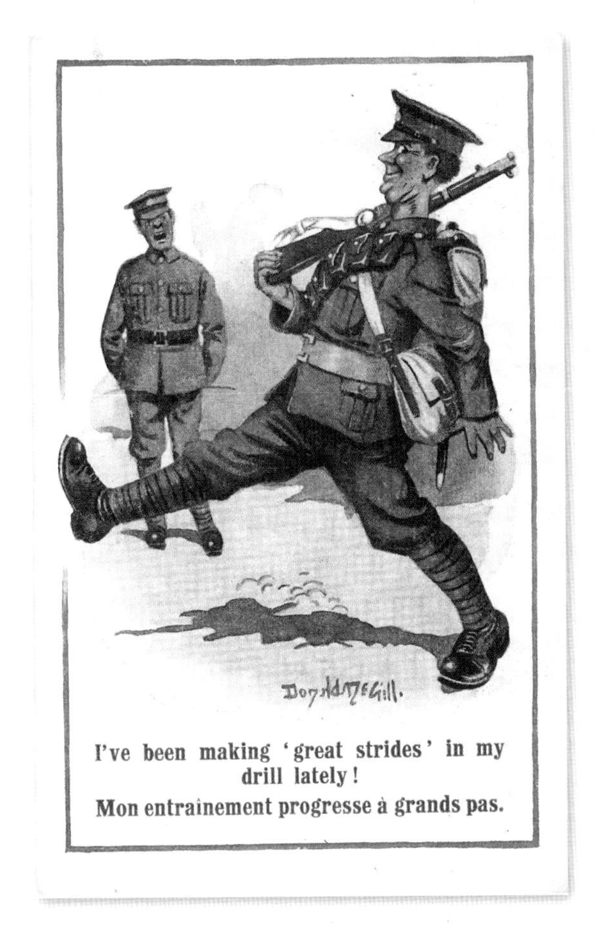

PLATE 148 'I'VE BEEN MAKING "GREAT STRIDES" IN MY DRILL LATELY!' (ALSO IN FRENCH)

During basic training, many hours were spent on drill. The card was stamped but not postmarked or dated. It was addressed to Miss A. Mitchell, The Lodge, Adhurst St Mary, Petersfield, Hants.

'Dear Alice. Thanks for PC Hope you are having a nice time and are feeling better. I have some news to tell you when you come back very nice news for me so long H.L.'

What was the very nice news? Had the writer been promoted?

PLATE 149 'I LOVE THE LIFE, BUT OH YOUR KIT!'

The card was sent from Mansfield on 1 November to Mrs J.G. Steele, 36 Fortune Green Road, West Hampstead, London.

> 'Just a PC to say I do not expect to be home next week. Everything has been put back a week owing to the fact that we have not finished our firing. The chaps who were going on Fri[day] will go next week & I the week after lets hope. I am rather afraid it will be a case of wait & see. I can tell you I am really wild about it. Tomorrow there is a Brigade route March. Letter follows first chance. Love Eric.'

A rare card in that it was sent on 8 March 1917 from an address in Great Britain to the front. Most communications to the front were by letter.

> 'To 12144 Gn J.G. Smith, Royal Marine Artillery, Heavy Liege Train, B.E.F. [British Expeditionary Force] c/o GPO London.
>
> So glad you are well and comfortable. I have written twice to this same address. Have you had them yet. We are having some mild weather again, plenty of rain, etc. We are still very busy spring cleaning , Edie helping us. She is going to Eastbourne soon. I think [she] wants Mum to go to. It will do her good won't it. Hope you are well. Yours Kit.'

Unlike McGill, Bruce Bairnsfather served on the Western Front from 1914 to 1915 as a Lieutenant in the 1st Warwickshire Regiment. Many of his cartoons from that time were published by the popular illustrated magazine *The Bystander*. Bairnsfather's 'Fragments from France', first published in February 1916, was an immediate success. More 'Fragments from France' were published between 1917 and 1919. From mid-1916 many of the cartoons first published by *The Bystander* were produced as postcards in nine series of six cards in illustrated presentation envelopes, priced at 8d. The five postcards below are all from the first 'Fragments from France' magazine. Although Bairnsfather's drawings are humorous, they tend to be sombre in colour. The cards were printed in England and concentrated on action at the front.

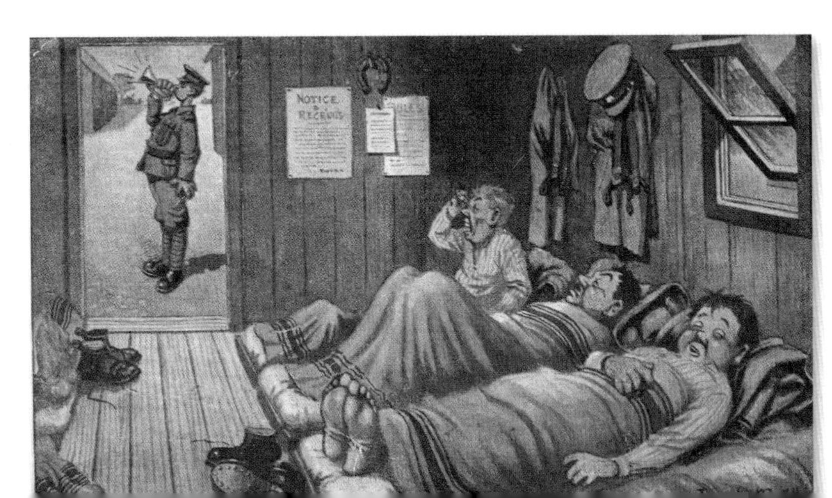

PLATE 151 KEEPING HIS HAND IN

Private Smith, the company bomber, formerly 'Shinio', the popular juggler, frequently caused considerable anxiety to the platoon.

The cards sent front Blandford Camp on 18 July 1916 by Leonard, who was in training, to Miss A. Frankland, 13 Brighton Place, Hunslet, Leeds.

'Dear Annie, Very many thanks for letter, cigs, tobacco and toffee, They are all A1 I hope you will like this card. I will forward the rest of the series later with love Leonard xxx'

The card is one of six in the first series, produced in mid-1916.

The card was sent from Clacton-on-Sea on 24 October 1916 by a father to his daughter, Miss Winnie Girbank, Tynedale, Arncliffe Terrace, Northallerton.

'Thanks for your letter I was very pleased to hear from you heaps of love Dad.'

The card is one of six in the fourth series.

PLATE 152 'THE PUSH' IN THREE CHAPTERS – BY ONE WHO'S BEEN 'PUSHED'

PLATE 153 A MAXIM MAXIM
'Fire should be withheld till a favourable target presents itself.'
The card, from the fourth series, was not postally used.

PLATE 154 MY DUG-OUT – A LAY OF THE TERRACES'

The card was sent by 'Jack' on 26 May 1917 to Mrs T. Smith, 35 Chelsea Road, Southsea, Hants.

> '26 May 1917
> Dear Ruth.
> Find my club card and see how much I owe and pay 1/6 subscription for me, as I think it must be time to pay again.
> Jack.'

The card was passed by a naval censor. Jack may well have been a senior naval officer used to giving commands. The card is one of six from the fourth series.

PLATE 155 A PROPOSAL IN FLANDERS

On a card from series 8 sent on 31 December 1918, days after the Armistice. 'Peter' writes:

> 'How well I can picture your smile when you look at picture on other side and so I think will "Mother".
>
> I have got a series, and they are all very good. May send you another or two later. My fond love to both of you and may the New Year bring you all the good fortune and happiness it is possible to have. Ever yours affectionately Peter.'

The cards produced from the drawings of Fergus Mackain were the work of a private soldier who also served at the front. Mackain produced four sets of cards portraying Tommy's life – 'In Training', 'At the Base', 'Up the Line' and 'Out on Rest'. There were ten cards in each set. The cards were first published in Boulogne in October 1917 by Imprimérie P. Gaulthier on thin card, and subsequently by the Paris firm Visé. The charming colour-washed cards display a deep understanding of what it was like to be a Tommy on the Western Front.

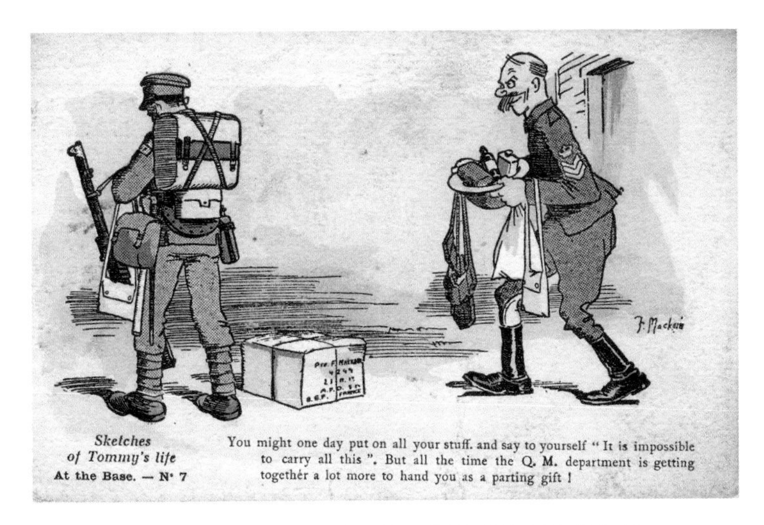

PLATE 156 SKETCHES OF TOMMY'S LIFE – 'AT THE BASE' (NO. 7)

'You might one day put on all your stuff. And say to yourself it is impossible to carry all this. But all the time the QM, Department is getting together a lot more to hand you as a parting gift!'

The card was not postally used.

PLATE 157 SKETCHES OF TOMMY'S LIFE – 'UP THE LINE' (NO. 1)

PLATE 157

'I got up early in the morning. Our train had gone as far as it was to go. As I was making tea in the dawn, I heard for the first time a sound like distant thunder... but it wasn't thunder.'

A very interesting card which may have been written in a trench at the front. The card is splattered with mud and the writing is difficult to read.

'Dear — just a few lines hoping to find you in best of health as it leaves me in the best at the present I am sending the cards for — as we shall be on — by — you get this lot so you must excuse me not writing now for a few days I must close best of —'

PLATE 158 BACK OF CARD

PLATE 159

The card was not dated and may well have been sent in an envelope to Miss Copping, Newton Road, Ipswich, Suffolk.

'Best wishes for the coming year. Love Stephen xxx'

PLATE 159 SKETCHES OF TOMMY'S LIFE – 'UP THE LINE' (NO. 7)
'One of the bright spots in our life.'

PLATE 160 SKETCHES OF TOMMY'S LIFE – 'OUT ON REST' (NO. 5)
'A regular carouse of coffee and fried eggs is one of the things we always have when we get to one of these villages.'
The card was not postally used.

THE BOY HERO OF THE BATTLE OF JUTLAND.
FOR VALOUR
H.M.S. VIVID
ENGLAND
EXPECTS
THAT
EVERY
MAN
WILL
DO
HIS
DUTY
Boy, First Class, JOHN TRAVERS CORNWELL. V.C. Died June 2nd 1916
Mortally wounded early in the action, he remained standing alone at a most exposed post quietly awaiting orders, until the end of the battle, with the gun's crew dead and wounded all round him.
Age, 16½ Years.

19 War at Sea

PLATE 161 THE BOY HERO OF THE BATTLE OF JUTLAND – BOY (FIRST CLASS) JOHN TRAVERS CORNWELL VC

Jack Cornwell was born on 8 January 1900 in Leyton, London. The son of Eli and Alice Cornwell, he was educated at Walton Road School, Manor Park. When war broke out, Eli Cornwell joined the army and Jack joined the Royal Navy. The younger Cornwell went through preliminary training at Devonport from 27 July 1915 and became a First Class Boy on HMS *Chester* for active service in Admiral Beatty's North Sea Squadron.

On 31 May 1916, during the Battle of Jutland, Cornwell was mortally wounded in action and died two days later in Grimsby hospital. He was posthumously awarded the Victoria Cross.

> 'John Travers Cornwell, Boy First Class, ONJ, 42563. Mortally wounded early in the action, Boy First Class John Travers Cornwell remained standing alone at a most exposed post, quietly awaiting orders, until the end of the action, with the gun's crew dead and wounded around him. His age was under sixteen and a half years.' (*London Gazette*, 15 September 1916)[18]

The flags around the card spell out 'England expects that every man will do his duty'.

PLATE 162 'GOD WHO MADE THEE MIGHTY, MAKE THEE MIGHTIER YET'

The card, not postally used, shows 'a mighty Dreadnought' and (from left to right): Sir John French, Commander of the Expeditionary Forces in 1914; Admiral Jellicoe, In Supreme Command of the Grand Fleet; and Lord Kitchener, Secretary of State for War, who was to perish with the sinking of HMS *Hampshire* on 5 June 1916.

In 1914 the strength of the United Kingdom lay with its navy, which was the strongest in the world and acted as a major deterrent to German naval ambitions. As a result, apart from some major engagements (including at Jutland), the large fleets kept their distance and many naval reservists were transformed into the soldiers of the Royal Naval Division.[19]

Joining the Jutland engagement, the bravery of a young boy sailor earned him Britain's highest military honour.

PLATE 163 'AND THE GREEN GRASS GREW ALL AROUND ME BOYS!'

The German Navy's limited involvement in the war at sea was mocked on a card 'The German Navy Taking Root!' On the back of the card the sender writes, 'Notice the cobwebs and spiders and birds nests.'

The involvement of German submarines did, however, pose a substantial threat to shipping. The recorded operational history of the submarine *U-8* with the German 1st Flotilla included a sortie into Heligoland Bight early on in the war and a single patrol from Belgium in which it sunk 15,049 tons of British shipping, including an aborted attack on the hospital ship *St Andrew*. However, the *U-8* was to become the first confirmed casualty of the First World War in English territorial waters.

PLATE 164 SINKING OF THE GERMAN SUBMARINE *U-8* BY A BRITISH DESTROYER

On 4 March 1915, the U-8 submarine was passing westwards through the Dover Strait when it ran into the nets of the Dover Barrage. Attempts to get clear attracted the attention of the drifter *Roburr*, which called up the destroyer patrol, a unit of the Royal Navy whose primary task was to prevent enemy German shipping, chiefly submarines, from entering the English Channel en route to the Atlantic Ocean. The destroyer HMS *Gurkha* lowered an explosive sweep, and when the line snagged on an underwater obstruction, the charge was fired. *U-8* was badly damaged and the commander ordered the submarine to surface, where U-8 was abandoned, though not before HMS *Gurkha* and HMS *Maori* had opened fire. According to the back of another postcard in the same series, the four officers and crew were all rescued.

At least three different cards show the German mine-laying submarine *UC-5*, captured in 1916.

Between July 1915 and April 1916, this submarine sank thirty-two vessels, including the hospital ship Anglia with the loss of 129 casualties and crew. On 27 April, while on mine-laying duties, *UC-5* was forced to surface and ran aground on Shipwash shoal in the Thames estuary. When the scuttling charges failed to explode, she was captured by HMS *Firedrake*. Later, she was towed up the Thames and then moored at Temple Pier, where the submarine stayed for three weeks, raising money for sailors' funds. It is said that over 200,000 visitors paid to see her.[20]

In an extract from a card posted on 15 August 1916, Grandma writes:

> 'Grandpa and I went to look at this submarine yesterday. A Charge of 6d for adults and 3d (for children) is made to each person. 1000's have been during this month. The money I believe goes to the sailor's fund.'[21]

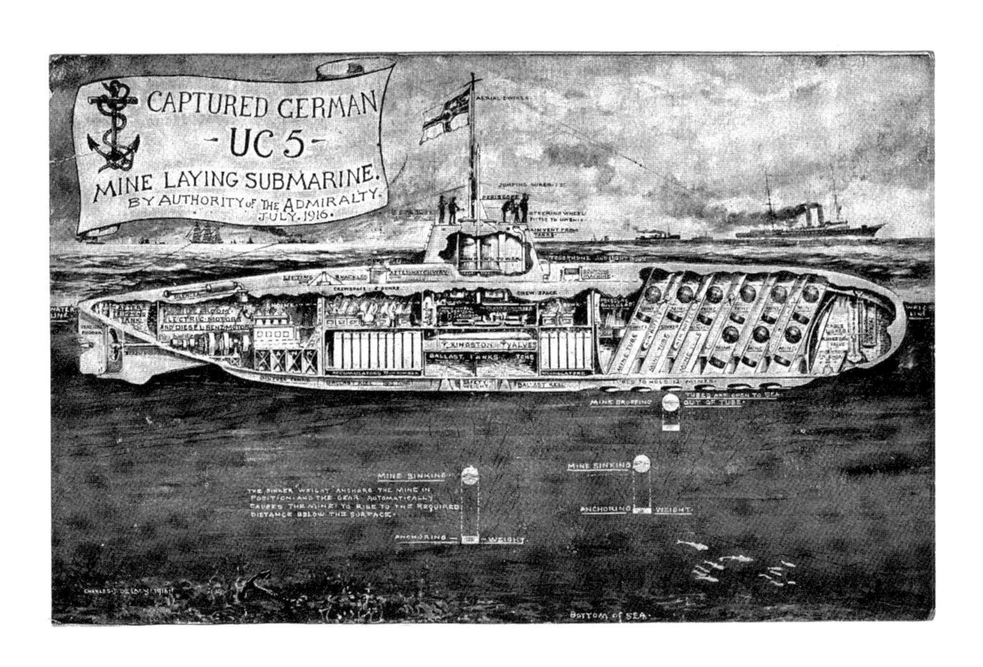

PLATE 166 GERMAN TRANSPORT SUNK BY A BRITISH SUBMARINE IN THE SEA OF MARMORA ON 3 JUNE 1915

A French card sent from New Cross (London) on 7 March 1916 to Miss W Purnell Jones, Warwickshire House, Gower Street, London.

'Thought perhaps you would like a card. Hope you're getting on better this week than last, I don't mind telling you that I have not moved from the fire this week, it has been so cold. With love K.C.'

PLATE 167 A STEAMER SUNK BY THE SUBMARINE *U-21*

On 5 September 1914, HMS *Pathfinder*, a small British cruiser, was torpedoed and sunk in the North Sea by *U-21*. This was the first warship to be sunk by a German U boat during the First World War. *U-21* took part in eleven patrols, during which she sank thirty-six ships with a total of 79,005 tons. The submarine, under the command of Otto Hersing, survived the war but was sunk in an accident on passage to surrender.

The numbers on the card refer to numbers on cards in a booklet about the raid on the port of Zeebrugge. This raid, on 22 and 23 April 1918, was an attempt by the Royal Navy to block the Belgian–Zeebrugge canal entrance to prevent German submarines based at Bruges from leaving port and causing a threat to Allied control of the English Channel and southern North Sea.

The view of the entrance to the canal shows two obsolete ships, *Intrepid* and *Iphigenia*, which were sunk in the narrowest part of the canal. A third ship, *Thetes*, did not make it to the canal entrance and was scuttled prematurely. The blockships were sunk in the wrong place and after a few days the Germans had opened the canal to submarines at high tide.

Vindictive and *Iris II* connected with the mole and landed a force of sailors and a battalion of Marines. The raid was a failure and British casualties very high. Of 700 men involved, over 200 were killed and over 350 wounded. In contrast, it was reported that German losses were very few in number. However, the Zeebrugge raid was promoted by Allied propaganda as a British victory and eight Victoria Crosses were awarded, including one to Richard Douglas Sandford, who was in command of submarine C3. He skilfully placed the vessel in between the piles of the viaduct before lighting a fuse and abandoning her. The viaduct was destroyed.[22]

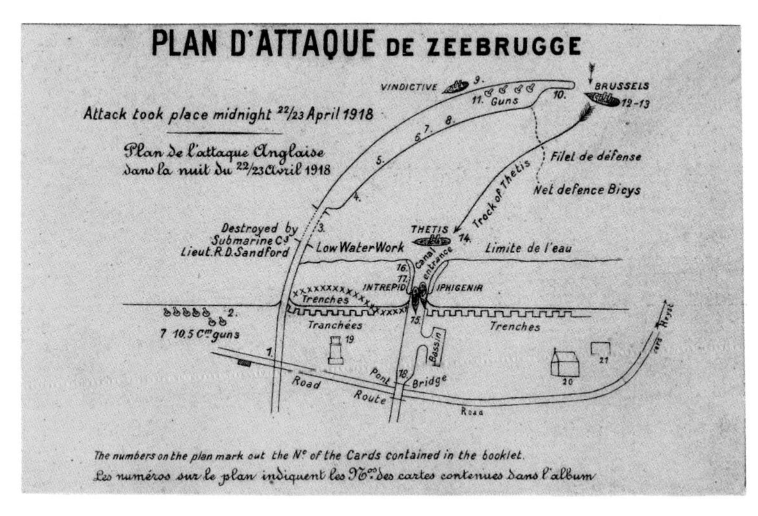

PLATE 169 OSTENDE – VESTIGE DU 'VINDICTIVE' – IN MORIAM (23 APRIL–10 MAY 1918)

The card, sent from Ostende on 8 September 1928 to Mrs H. Allcorn, The Chestnuts, Herstmonceaux, Sussex, features a memorial to *Vindictive*, which played a major part in the Zeebrugge raid on 22 and 23 April 1918, and was later used as a block ship during an attack on Ostende on 9 and 10 May 1918.

'Jack & Kitty' wrote:

> 'Dear Mother. Hope to be home to morrow night. It has been a hectic week, as we have been in 4 countries – England, Belgium, France & Holland. Quite a record. Still very hot here. Love Jack & Kitty.'

It is interesting to note that the rector of the church in Herstmonceaux sent a card on 19 December 1918 to 104442 Private J.H. Allcorn, No. 3 Section, 16th Labour Cor., B.E.F. France.

20 War in the Air

DEATH AND DAMAGE to property inflicted on the British civilian population during the First World War was not substantial, especially when compared with what was to come during the Second World War.

In December 1914, the German Navy carried out attacks against the British east coast towns of Scarborough, Hartlepool and Whitby. The shelling of these town resulted in 137 dead and 590 wounded.[23,24,25]

PLATE 170 THE RAIDER

A card, not postally used, shows a Zeppelin caught in search lights. In reality, anti-aircraft guns lacked the range to shoot them down.

Everything changed on the night of 2 September 1916 when Lieutenant William Leefe Robinson of the Royal Flying Corps machine-gunned Zeppelin SL11 with the new incendiary bullets, setting it alight. This was the first 'kill' over British soil. Robinson was awarded the Victoria Cross but was later shot down himself over France and spent the last year of the war as a POW. Sadly, after his release, Robinson died of influenza in December 1918.[26]

The French and the Belgians also produced postcards depicting downed Zeppelins.

THE RAIDER.
PUBLICATION SANCTIONED BY OFFICIAL PRESS BUREAU
Publishing Office
39, St. Andrew's Hi[illegible] E.C.
(Copyright)

On a card sent from Newcastle upon Tyne on 19 September 1918, some four years after the event, Alice wrote:

> 'Dear Mother, Received P.C. with thanks, we are changing our lodgings on Sat. so I will write you on Sunday. We are nearer to the works, & cheaper so that is better for us & quite clean & cosy. Ta ta love to all your loving Daughter and Son. Alice & George.'

Cards of the shelling of Hartlepool may have been on sale in Newcastle, which is a few miles north of the town and where Alice and George may have been on war work.

The first air attacks on Britain came from Zeppelin airships, which bombed the east coast in January 1915. Raids on London followed at the end of May. The advantage of the Zeppelins was in sowing fear and anxiety in the civilian population.

The anxiety was also felt by those serving at the front. On a card sent home in 1915, Jim wrote:

> 'I heard that you have had another Zep raid and all had a rare fright. Whenever are they going to bring one down to put a stop to them.'

BOMBARDMENT OF WEST HARTLEPOOL. Back view of house in Rugby Terrace.

PLATE 172 AERIAL WAR – BRABANT-LE-ROI (MEUSE) – GERMAN MURDERERS' CRAFT

The card, which was not postally used, depicts the front and a branch of the helix of the Zeppelin LZ 77, which was brought down on 21 February 1916 at 8.47 p.m. by the Auto-Canons Section of Revigny. It reportedly took over twenty shots from the anti-aircraft guns to bring the Zeppelin down.

Artistic licence has been used to show 'The Zeppelin brought down in Celle road at Badonviller and coming from Strasbourg.' The card was not postally used.

During the second half of the war, the German bomber aircraft, the Goth IV, operated from airfields in Belgium, mostly in the area around Ghent, and attacked London and the Home Counties east of the capital.

On a card posted from Bexleyheath (Greater London) on 10 July 1917, Molly wrote: 'We had a dreadfull air-raid over hear.'

Although the Goth IV had a range of over 400 miles and delivered over 1,100 pound bombs, few raids could be carried out successfully further to the west. The British airfields were also to be found around London and close to the coast in Kent and Essex.

Fighter and bomber pilots were in action at the front, but the most important role was that of reconnaissance and surveillance. Both sides did their best to disrupt flying over their lines and over no man's land.

PLATE 174 ANTI-AIRCRAFT GUNNERS 'SPOTTING' A HUN PLANE

The card, one of the *Daily Mail* official war pictures (series 14, no. 105), has on the back:

> 'An exciting moment at the Front. These anti-aircraft gunners have spotted a German aeroplane, and are hurriedly sighting and aiming their gun.'

It is interesting to note that the card was sent to a young child.

> 'My dear Edna,
> It was very nice of you to spare me a Photo, also a bit of love & kisses. & I hear Father Christmas was most kind in bringing you lots of presents. I am sure you are a very lucky little Girlie. Love & kisses from Aunt Caroline.'

PLATE 175 BELGIAN ANTI-AIRCRAFT GUNNERS
The card, not postally used, was sold in aid of the YMCA Hut Fund 'to provide Comforts, Shelter and Recreation for our soldiers' (see also plates 95 and 146).

PLATE 176 THE KING INSPECTING ROYAL NAVAL AIR SERVICE OFFICERS

The card, one of the *Daily Mail* official war pictures (series 13, no. 100), has on the back:

> 'Among the King's meetings with his troops on the Western Front was this quiet inspection of a number of officers of the Royal Naval Air Service.'

As a result of the German Navy's limited involvement in the war (see plate 171), many men who had joined the British Navy ended up fighting on land or in the Royal Flying Corps.

PLATE 177 THE FIRST RECRUIT OF THE ROYAL FLYING CORPS

The card was sent from Bedford on 20 June 1917 to Master H. Pullan, Wilden Rectory, Beds:

'With love from Chris.'

Master Hugh Pullan was the only child of Reverend John Richard Pullan and his wife Mary Charlotte. Hugh was just 6 years old when the card was sent to him. He never served in the armed forces.

PLATE 178 FOR FATHERLAND

21 Cards of the Central Powers

THE CARDS SENT by those serving with the Central Powers (including Germany, Austria, Hungary, Turkey and Bulgaria) were not so different from those sent by the Allies during the war. However, unlike the French, there were no cards showing damage to buildings and few cards that made fun of the enemy.

PLATE 179 'WHAT SHOULD I WRITE TO YOU?'

On the back of a card sent on 15 June 1916 from an address in Austria, a young woman asks:

'What should I write to you, dearest friend, who is so far away, but always close? I always want to stay yours, God protect you! Victory!'

PLATE 178

The card was sent on 19 September from Bayreuth, a town north-east of Nuremberg and close to the border with Czechoslovakia.

'Let my wound heal quickly
I have to go back into the fight.
Whoever wants to, when
Germany's honour is at stake,
Doesn't want to be on the
battlefield.'

PLATE 180 SOLDIERS WRITING HOME

This Feldpostkarte (field postcard), not postally used, shows four German soldiers writing home. On the back of the card it states:

'Der Europaische Krieg 1914/15'

('The European War 1914/15')

As with many French cards, the dates of the war were changed as the length of hostilities increased.

PLATE 181 LOOK AT US

A photograph, sent as a postcard on 23 March 1916, shows six soldiers sitting outside their bunker.

PLATE 182 ATTACK ON ANTWERP, BELGIUM

The card, which was not postally used, is one of a set used to forecast what Germany would do at the start of hostilities. At least two cards in the set were posted in December 1914, one of which shows an attack on England by the German fleet supported by Zeppelins.

PLATE 183 POUR LES BOCHES!
This patriotic card was not postally used. Pictures of children were even used to show contempt for the enemy.

22 The French Riposte

PLATE 184 LE CHIEN SANITAIRE ... ET PATRIOTE! ('THE SANITARY AND PATRIOTIC DOG!')

The French were happy to use lavatorial humour when making fun of the enemy. Several cards depict Red Cross dogs showing contempt for Germany.

PLATE 185 CHASSE A L'INTRUS ('CHASE THE INTRUDER')

PLATE 185

The card was passed by the sensor. Five birds representing the Allies are shown chasing and attacking the bird representing Germany, who had invaded their lands. The card was sent on 5 May 1916 to Miss F. Yeomans, South Street, Chailey, near Lewes, Sussex:

> 'My own dearest Floss
> many many thanks for lovely letter just received dated 27 (April). I was so pleased to hear that you are quite well. Take great care of yourself. I am pleased to say I am quite well. Duck Old Fritz has had another fresh supply of ammunition I think for he has been throwing them about rather-- but he has had about twice the amount-- please give my fondest loved to dear Mum. Good night fondest love and heaps of X I remain your ever Y L Bro? May 1st 1916 Somewhere in France.'

Could 'Y L Bro' be 'Your Loving Brother'?

PLATE 186 APRÈS LA VICTOIRE
The card, posted on 6 September 1918, shows the departure of the Emperor Franz Josef in a cart drawn by the Kaiser – soon France will have the victory!

PLATE 187 CONTEMPT FROM BORDEAUX
The French girl, to register her contempt, thumbs her nose at the German, who is being restrained by children representing Russia, Scotland and Belgium. The card was not dated or postally used, but on the back is written 'To Charlie from Dad.'

PLATE 188 LANGAGE DES TIMBRES DES ALLIES

Bert wrote to Miss Nell Draper, Blackpan Cottages, Newport Road, Lake, Sandown, Isle of Wight, England:

> 'My dearest Nell,
> Just another card for you. The language of the stamps of the Allies. The one Heroism is Montenegro and the one Courage is Serbia. The others you will know.
> With all love Bert'

On the card, Britain is labelled: 'VALEUR' ('valour'), France 'HONNEUR' ('honour'), Russia 'GRANDEUR' ('grandeur'), Belgium 'BRAVOURE' ('bravery') and Italy 'GLOIRE' ('glory').

A card written by Private Harry Shore, 2nd Essex Regt., B.E.F. on 8 November 1915 was passed by the censor and sent to Miss A Ryder, Fairfax House, Church Road, South Farnborough, Hants.

> 'Just a card to let you know I am still in good health as I was very pleased to hear you are A1 I got two letters from you yesterday so I will write you a good long letter tonight. Fondest love to all from Harry.'

The French stamps have 'A VOUS MA VIE' ('To you my life'), 'AMITIE' ('friendship'), 'ESPEREZ' ('hope'), 'BAISERS' ('kisses'), 'A BIENTOT' ('See you soon'), 'PENSEZ A MOI' ('Think of me'), 'AMOUR ARDENT' ('ardent love') and 'JE VOUS AIME' ('I love you'). As Harry was on active service, there was no stamp on the card.

PLATE 190 'MES PENSEES SONT AVEC VOUS!' ('MY THOUGHTS ARE WITH YOU')

A sentimental card sent on 7 July 1915 by Ned Brand to his wife, who may well have been working at Keith Hall, Inveraray, Scotland. Soldiers used the cards that they could purchase locally, and very many sentimental cards were sent to wives and girlfriends back home (see plates 46 and 78).

> 'Dear Jeannie, got your letter glad to hear of your entertainment but there will be too quiet a lot now for its roasting here just now. Wasn't there a little trinket in the letter with PC. I'm getting a motorbike when I come home. Im OK and send my best love and xxx Ned.'

Pinx. A. Beerts. L'Ange de la tranchée. VISÉ PARIS
The angel of the trench. 2392.
А. Бэртсъ. Покровительница траншей. I. M. L.

PLATE 191 THE ANGEL OF THE TRENCH

The card was sent from Cannes, in the south of France, on 11 September 19(?). The caption is written in French, English and Russian. Both when in training and when at the front, servicemen were delighted to receive parcels from their family or well-wishers.

PLATE 192 INSTRUCTING COMPANY

The card was posted on 29 June 1918 from Hancock Branch, Augusta, Georgia, to Miss Cecile Doucet, Box 792, Claremont, New Hampshire.

The message on the back was written in French.

['Dear Cissie,
I am on guard this evening. I will send you a letter tonight because you have to play games to see which companion is the best one of twelve hundred and fifty soldiers here Good Bye.']

It is not clear why the card was written in French.

23 America Joins the War

On 2 April 1917, US President Woodrow Wilson went before a Joint Session of Congress to request a declaration of war against Germany. Wilson cited Germany's violation of its pledge to suspend unrestricted submarine warfare in the North Atlantic and the Mediterranean, as well as its attempts to entice Mexico into an alliance against the United States, as his reasons for declaring war.

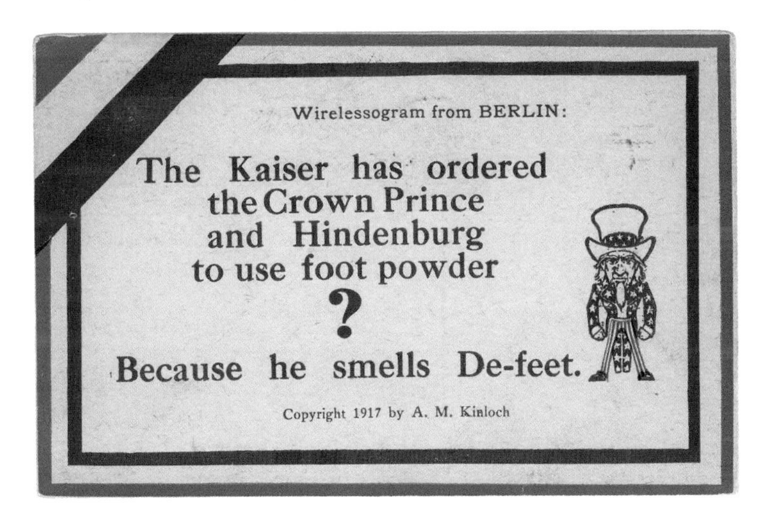

PLATE 193 THE KAISER HAS ORDERED

The card was posted on 16 May 1918 from Detroit to Mr H.L. Snyders, Boston, Mass, Commonwealth Pier, Stringham Dep.

'H.L.S.
Dear Friend: – sure takes you a longtime to answer that letter. I go to camp the 28* (May) and I think it will be to Georgia. Hope I get a few Huns. S'

PLATE 194 THE ARSENAL AT BREST

The card was sent on 14 June 1919 by Private R.R. Coudert of the US Army to Mrs Doubleday, 27 The Terrace, Barnes, London, England.

> 'Arrived here today on my way home. Will write when I get on other side. Pte. R.R. Coudert. U.S. Army'

Private Coudert may well have sailed from Brest to the United States. For him, the war was over and he would be back home for Christmas 1919.

24 Letters from France

THE VAST MAJORITY of families of soldiers who were killed or wounded in France were notified not by telegrams, but by a letter posted in a buff-coloured envelope with OHMS (On His Majesty's Service) printed on the outside. Telegrams were sent almost exclusively to the next of kin of officers. When writing to the deceased soldier's family, platoon officers and friends of the soldier made every effort to soften the blow by using phrases such as 'sadness at the loss of a fine soldier', 'death was instantaneous and he could have felt no pain', 'buried along with his comrades'. This is well demonstrated in a letter sent by Sister E.M. Lyle to Mr Hodgkiss:

> 'XI C.C.S.
> France
> 8/10/17
>
> Dear Mr Hodgkiss
> You will have received the sad news of the loss of your son 35451 Sergt J.A. Hodgkiss R.F.A. and I am just writing to give you all the particulars I know.
>
> He was admitted on the 5th very ill indeed, with a wound of buttock & a severe penetrating of abdomen. Everything possible was done for him but he passed away at 3pm on the 6th inst: He did not talk or speak of anything, except now and again he asked for anything he wanted. He did not realize his condition but I told him that I would write to you as soon as I could get a few minutes and would send his love & he seemed glad. He was very drowsy all of the time, & suffered very little actual pain. He was unconscious for some time before the end which was very peaceful. He will be laid to rest in the Cemetery here, by the side of his comrades. Any personal effects must be sent to the Record Office & forwarded

from there to you.

Please accept my sympathy for you in your trouble.

Yours Truly
E.M.Lyle
Sister in Charge'

Joseph Arthur Hodgkiss enlisted in Buxton, Derbyshire and served in the Royal Horse Artillery. He was in the Royal Field Auxiliary (RFA) in 1914 with the rank of Corporal. Later that year, Hodgkiss was promoted to Acting Sergeant, probably due to casualties in the unit. This acting role ended in 1916 and he reverted to Corporal. Hodgkiss was promoted to Substantive Sergeant in 1917 but died in XI Casualty Clearing Station in France on 6 October 1917.

PLATE 195 PHOTO OF 2ND LIEUTENANT RICHARD (DICK) PATRICK WILMOT GETHIN, 2ND ROYAL MUNSTER FUSILIERS (12 DECEMBER 1914)

At the end of September 1915, Mrs Clemence Gethin received a telegram – her only child, Richard, had been killed in action during the battle of Loos. She had already lost her husband, Captain Henry Gethin.

Dick Gethin was educated at Hodder Preparatory School and Stonyhurst College. It was said that he was a young man of 'mighty stature'. Dick Gethin entered Sandhurst in August 1914 on a King's Cadetship, to which he was entitled following the death of his father, Captain Henry Gethin, who had been killed in action in South Africa in 1900. He was gazetted to the Munster Fusiliers in November 1914, but was killed in action, aged just 19 years old, on 26 September 1915 during the battle of Loos. He is buried at Dud Corner Cemetery, Loos.

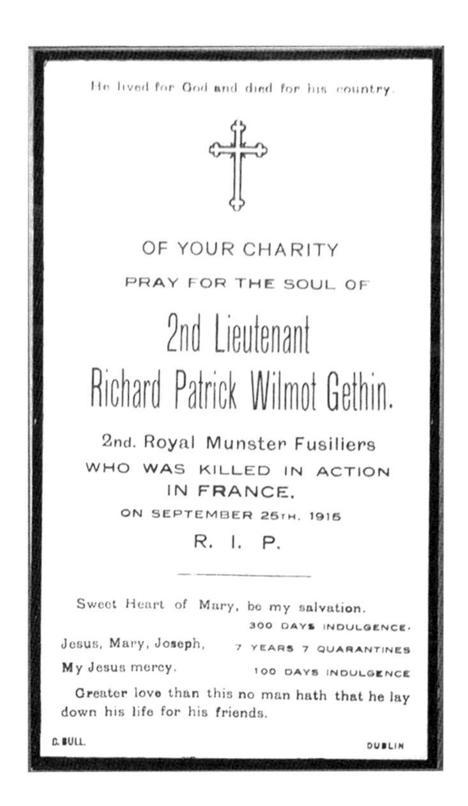
He lived for God and died for his country.

OF YOUR CHARITY
PRAY FOR THE SOUL OF

2nd Lieutenant
Richard Patrick Wilmot Gethin.

2nd. Royal Munster Fusiliers
WHO WAS KILLED IN ACTION
IN FRANCE.
ON SEPTEMBER 25TH. 1915
R. I. P.

Sweet Heart of Mary, be my salvation.
300 DAYS INDULGENCE.
Jesus, Mary, Joseph, 7 YEARS 7 QUARANTINES
My Jesus mercy. 100 DAYS INDULGENCE
Greater love than this no man hath that he lay down his life for his friends.

C. BULL DUBLIN

PLATE 196 HE LIVED FOR GOD AND DIED FOR HIS COUNTRY

Sometimes there was good news, as seen in this letter from 9 June 1918 from Maude to Kitty, 135 Bidston Avenue.

'My dear Kitty,
Thanks for your prompt reply to my PC. I was glad to hear from you again & to know that you are all well. I could not have written a letter last week no matter how important it had been I was so worried over Harold – I went about doing most unnecessary things & leaving everything else alone. On the Monday the battle started (May 27th) I had an awful fit of the blues & could not make out what was the matter as there was no news in the paper – all was quiet where Harold was (Barry au bac) & he said in one of his letters that there was scarcely a shot fired day & night. He said the heat was terrific & many of the men had gone in hospital with fever – water was very scarce & he could not have a decent wash or a change of clothes until he came out of the line in a month's time. When I saw that the offensive had started I could not believe it was down south near Rheims & my heart sank lower and lower as I knew Harold would get the first onrush as he was in charge of a Battery. On June 5th I received a field card from him saying he was wounded & I felt like standing on my head with joy as I had been thinking I would never see him again and imagining all kinds of horrible things. The following day I had two more cards & this morning the long looked for letter arrived & I felt at peace with the world. Harold had lost everything except what he stood up in, but he says he still has his fountain pen (a self filler I bought him for his birthday), golliwog, which Marjorie sent him, & our latest photograph taken the day before he left for France this last time. I will give you a portion of his letter in his own words:-

"I am quite safe now but on 29th May, when the Bosche advanced without us having the slightest idea of a push, my guns were all blown to pieces in the terrible bombardment – all my men are gone, too, & I am as far as I know the only one left in the whole Battery, except the O.C. [officer commanding], who was in hospital with trench fever. I was taken prisoner for 2 hours but escaped & fought my way through being wounded in the neck with shrapnel. I found my way to the hospital where my wound was dressed but I had to leave there at 1am next morning because the Bosche had advanced rapidly and were just outside the village. I was put in charge of 66 wounded men (walking cases like myself) & we have been marching ever since & have done over 100 miles sleeping in the fields all night with covering. It was the thoughts of your distress that made me break away from the Bosch for it was simply asking for death & although my clothes are ripped here and there with bullets and I had to swim across the river with them after me I am still smiling."

You will see that he has had another miraculous escape and it is only a month since his last narrow shave. I do feel relieved I can tell you but the worst of it is he will be in the thick of It – again as soon as he is fit. You ought to thank your stars you have still your husband at home – I never knew what worry was till Harold went to France & some days I fell 100 years old with all that is happening round about.'

Could it be that Harold was inclined to exaggerate the danger and his bravery?

Examples of censor marks

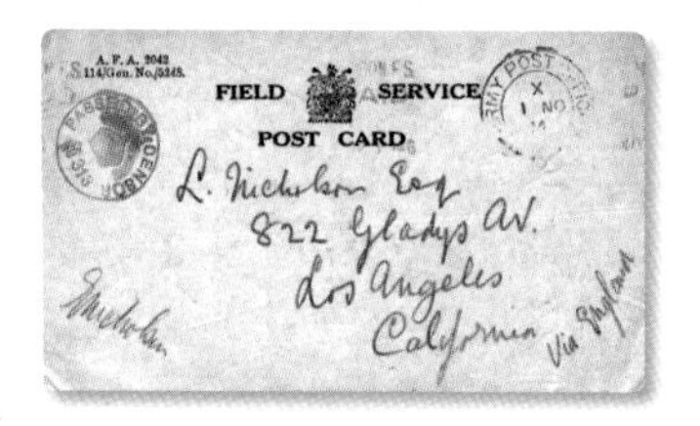

Small red circular handstamp, example 1 November 1914

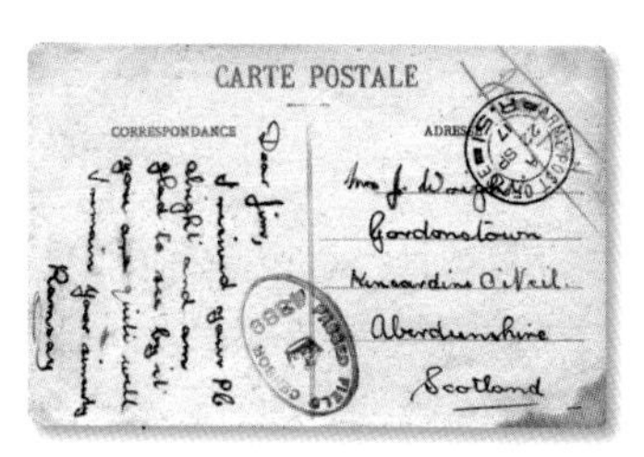

Oval example, 22 September 1917

Square example, 14 August 1915,

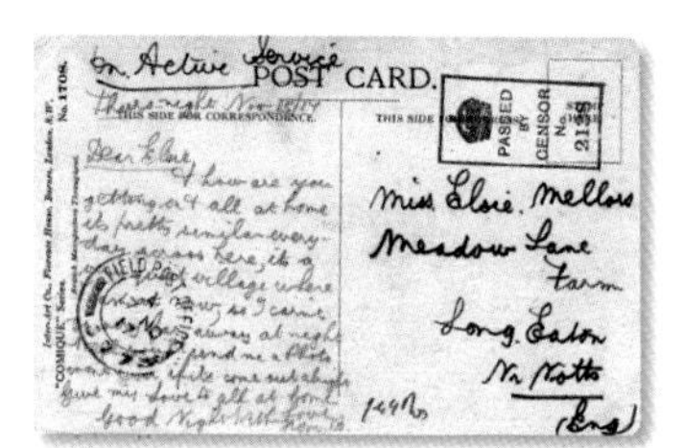

Rectangular handstamp example, 17 November 1917

Triangular example, 29 April 1915

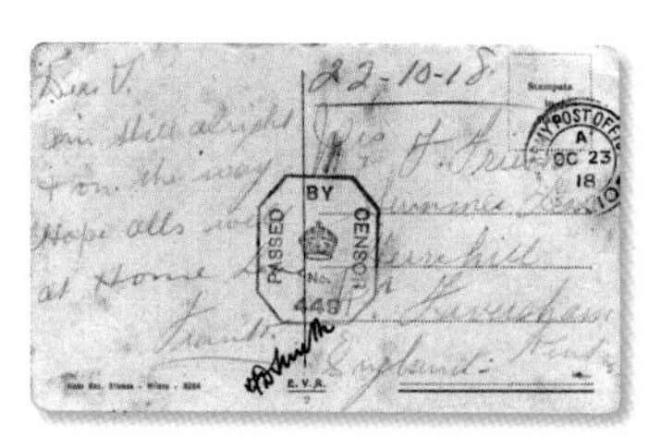

Octagonal handstamp example, 23 October 1918

Hexagonal example, 4 September 1916

Shield handstamp example, 17 December 1918

Acknowledgements

The estate of Captain Bruce Bairnsfather for permission to use plates 159, 160, 161, 162 and 163.

The estate of Private Fergus Mackain for permission to use plates 164, 165, 166, 167 and 168.

Brian Lund, collector and editor of *Picture Postcard Monthly*.

Andrew Brooks, collector, for information on field service postcards and censor stamps.

Michael Partridge, archivist at Eastbourne College, and Peter Duckers from the Shropshire Museum, for research into the life of Russell Llewellyn Mandeville Lloyd.

Barry Lane for research into the lives of Private Alfred Lifton, Private Thomas Cornell and Sergeant Joseph Hodgkiss.

Trevor N. Stewart for his research into the life of Master Hugh Pullan.

Elizabet Foy for the donation of letters sent during the First World War.

Beverley Stedman for providing silk postcard plates 81 and 82.

Geoff Ashton for research into the location of villages featured in French postcards.

Andy King of the *Daily Telegraph* for information relating to the Anti-German League.

Simon Evers for transcription of the manuscript and Helen Wilton for proof-reading the manuscript.

References

[1] *The Times A Century in Photography*, p. 43.
[2] Van Emden & Humphries (2003), p. 9.
[3] Van Emden & Humphries (2003), p. 78.
[4] Lund (2014), plate 31.
[5] Holt & Holt (2014), p. 93 and plate 195.
[6] E. Buckland (1984), p. 88.
[7] Holt & Holt (2014), p. 136 and plate 272.
[8] De Vries (2014), p. 65.
[9] Dr Anne Carden-Coyne, quoted in Jenkins (2012).
[10] Wilton (2014), p. 41
[11] Brunt & Brunt (2013), p. 16.
[12] Wilton (1991), p. 13.
[13] Brunt & Brunt (2013), p. 35.
[14] Doyle (2010), pp. 43–4.
[15] Doyle (2010), pp. 46–7.
[16] Van Emden & Humphries (2003), pp. 254–5.
[17] Doyle (2010), pp. 36–7.
[18] Creagh & Humphris (eds) (2009), p. 217.
[19] Doyle (2010), pp. 10–11.
[20] Holt & Holt (2014), plate 312.
[21] Brooks (2014), p. 99.
[22] Burns (1991), p. 274.
[23] Holt & Holt (2014), plate 481.
[24] Van Emden & Humphries (2003), pp. 34–51.
[25] Doyle (2010), pp. 52–3.
[26] Doyle (2010), p. 53.

The Next of Kin Memorial Plaque (also known as the 'death penny') was a bronze plaque inscribed with the name of someone who died serving with the British and Empire forces. It was issued to the Next of Kin of the casualty along with a memorial scroll. A 'King's message' was enclosed with both, containing a facsimile signature of the King.

Bibliography, Sources and Further Reading

Arthur, Max, *Last Post: The Final Word from our First World War Soldiers* (London: Cassell, 2005).

Bairnsfather, Captain Bruce, *The Bystander's Fragments from France*, vols 1–7 (London: The Bystander, 1916–19).

Brooks, Andrew, *Postcard Messages from the Great War 1914–1919* (2014).

Brunt, Lloyd & Brunt, Mary, *The Blue Boys of World War I* (East Dean & Friston Local History Group, 2013).

Buckland, Elfreda, *The World of Donald McGill* (London: Blandford Press, 1984).

Buckland, Katherine, Heritage Office at Eastbourne Borough Council pamphlet (n.d.).

Burns, Ross, *The World War I Album* (London: Saturn Books Ltd, 1991).

Calder-Marshall, Arthur, *Wish You Were Here: The Art of Donald McGill* (London: Hutchinson, 1966).

Cox, Michael, *Women at War* (First World War series no. 7) (Keyworth: Reflections of a Bygone Age, 2014).

Creagh, Sir O'Moore & Humphris, E.M., *The V.C. and D.S.O Book: The Victoria Cross 1856–1920* (London: The Standard Art Book Co. Ltd, 2009).

Crossley, Bernard, *Donald McGill Postcard Artist* (Greaves & Thomas, 2014).

De Vries, Dr Guus, *The Great War through Picture Postcards* (Barnsley: Pen and Sword, 2014).

Doyle, Peter, *British Postcards of the First World War* (London: Shire Publications, 2010).

Doyle, Peter, *The British Soldier of the First World War* (London: Shire Publications, 2008).

Doyle, Peter & Foster, Chris, *What Tommy Took to War 1914–1918* (London: Shire Publications, 2014).

Ellis, John & Cox, Michael (eds), *The World War I, Databook: The Essential Facts and Figures for all the Combatants* (London: Aurum Press, 1993).

Holt, Tonie & Holt, Valmai, T*he Biography of Captain Bruce Bairnsfather* (Barnsley: Pen and Sword, 2014).

Holt, Tonie & Holt, Valmai, *Till the Boys Come Home: The First World War through Its Picture Postcards* (Barnsley: Pen and Sword, 2014).

Jenkins, Russell, 'How flirting, cross dressing and pantos healed Great War's love starved wounded', *The Times*, 26 December 2012.

Lund, Brian, *Faces of the First World War* (First World War series no. 5) (Keyworth: Reflections of a Bygone Age, 2014).

Lund, Brian, *Joining Up: Oh We Don't Want to Lose You* (First World War series no. 2) (Keyworth: Reflections of a Bygone Age, 2014).

Lund, Brian, *Patriotism: My Country Right or Wrong* (First World War series no. 1) (Keyworth: Reflections of a Bygone Age, 2014).

Lund, Brian, *Propaganda in the First World War* (First World War series no. 6) (Keyworth: Reflections of a Bygone Age, 2014).

Mackain, Private Fergus, *A Tommy's Life in the Trenches: A Soldier-Artist on the Western Front* (Stroud: Amberley, 2006).

Mackay, James A., Mussell, Philip & Mussell, John W. (eds), *Medal Yearbook* (Exeter: Token Publishing, 2008).

Ross, Stewart, *World War I Atlas of Conflicts* (Milwaukee, WI: Gareth Stevens Publishing, 2004).

The Times – A Century in Photography: A Portrait of Britain, 1900–1999 (London: Times Books, 1999).

Van Emden, Richard & Humphries, Steve, *All Quiet on the Home Front: An Oral History of Life in Britain During the First World War* (Barnsley: Pen and Sword, 2003).

Wilton, John & Smith, John, *A Portrait in Old Picture Postcards* (v.1) (Eastbourne) (Seaford: SB Publications, 1990).

Wilton, John, *A Second Portrait in Old Picture Postcards* (v.2) (Eastbourne) (Seaford: SB Publications, 1991).

Wilton, John & Howden, Chris, *Eastbourne Then and Now* (Seaford: SB Publications, 1999).

Wilton, John, *Eastbourne's French Connection* (Chippenham: Antony Rowe Publishing Services, 2005).

Wilton, John Paul, *McGill's War: A History of Life in Britain During the Great War: Illustrated by the Art of Donald Fraser McGill* (Brighton: FireStep Press, 2014).

POST CARD.

BUY NATIONAL WAR BONDS NOW

WAR BOND CAMPAIGN

ISSUED IN CONNECTION

WAR SAVINGS CO

CORRESPONDENCE ONLY

27 MAY 18

O.A.S. POST-CARD

PASSED

CARTE POSTALE

La Correspondance au recto n'est pas acceptée par tous les pays étrangers.

CORRESPONDANCE

ARMY RECREATION HUT

FIELD POST OFFICE

9 JA 16

A. F. A. 2042

Gen. No./5248.

Signature only.

FIELD

POST CARD

CARTE

CORRESPONDANCE